KT-171-818

There is a light that shines beyond all things on Earth,
beyond us all, beyond the heavens,
beyond the highest, the very highest heavens.
This is the radiant light that shines in the heart of man.

Chandogya Upanishad, 3.13.7

The TIGER *and the* ACROBAT

SUSANNA
TAMARO

Translated by
Nicoleugenia Prezzavento
and
Vicki Satlow

A Oneworld Book

First published in North America, Great Britain and Australia
by Oneworld Publications, 2017

Originally published in Italian as *La Tigre e l'Acrobata*
by La nave di Teseo, 2016

Copyright © Susanna Tamaro, 2016
English translation copyright © Nicoleugenia Prezzavento
and Vicki Satlow, 2017

The moral right of Susanna Tamaro to be identified as the
author of this work has been asserted by her in accordance
with the Copyright, Designs and Patents Act 1988

This is a work of fiction. Names, characters, places, and
incidents are either the product of the author's imagination or are used
fictitiously, and any resemblance to actual persons, living or dead,
businesses, companies, events or locales is entirely coincidental.

All rights reserved
Copyright under Berne Convention
A CIP record for this title is available from the British Library

ISBN 978-1-78607-282-5
eISBN 978-1-78607-283-2

Typeset by Fakenham Prepress Solutions, Fakenham, Norfolk NR21 8NN
Printed and bound in Great Britain by Clays Ltd, St Ives plc

Oneworld Publications
10 Bloomsbury Street
London WC1B 3SR
England

Northamptonshire
Libraries & Information
Services
NW

Askews & Holts

CHAPTER ONE

A Sliver of Light

Little Tiger was ushered into the world on a bed of leaves deep within a den, welcomed by the earthy scents of her mother and the forest.

Little Tiger was not Shere Khan: she knew nothing of the gauzy mists of the tropics or the carefree laziness inspired by that climate. She was born in the Far North, between the Arctic tundra and the snowy forests of the taiga, which stretches out from the West to the Far East, where the sun has risen since the beginning of time. She was more familiar with the huts of the Siberian shamans than with snake charmers.

Her mother had long, thick fur, extraordinarily long whiskers and a soft, warm body. There was nothing to fear as long as she could hear her mother's deep, regular breathing.

For the first few days, Little Tiger did nothing but suckle, curled up against her mother's side.

There was someone else close to her who suckled just like her, and to whom she clung every night in her sleep.

One morning, as Little Tiger roused from her sleep, something incredible happened. A sliver of light appeared in the darkness that had engulfed her since birth. It was faint, but was just bright enough to show her that as well as the Inside there was also an Outside. An Outside made of shadows, of dark shapes and silhouettes.

Something out there was moving.

The silhouettes soon turned into shapes and these shapes had a face. The face was that of her mother, who was licking her with her huge, rough tongue, almost flipping her over.

'Where am I?' was the first question Little Tiger asked.

'You're in our den,' Mother replied.

'And where was I before?'

'Before, you were inside my belly, with your brother.'

Inside the den, everything was familiar: the fallen tree trunks that made up the roof, the soft bed of leaves under her belly, the light that filtered through the tangled roots. But while the leaves and trunks were always there, the light came and went as it pleased. Sometimes it was there, sometimes it wasn't.

'Why does it do that?' she asked her mother.

'Because there is a time for the sun and a time for the stars.'

'Is the sun a tiger?'

Mother remained silent for a while. 'Yes,' she answered, 'because the sun is the King of the Sky.'

'Are we Kings too?' Little Tiger asked.

'Yes, we are Kings and Queens. The sun rules the sky and we rule the taiga.'

'So what?' Tiger Cub pressed.

'Everyone fears us and we fear no one.'

The third thing that Little Tiger discovered were her ears. One morning, as the sun seeped into the den, her attention was captured by a series of wonderful sounds.

To better understand where they came from, she got up on her wobbly legs and started tottering towards the light. As she was about to peek outside, her mother's imposing body blocked the entrance.

'Why aren't you inside with your brother?' she roared, grabbing her by the scruff of her neck and carrying her back to the rear of the den. 'You're not allowed outside without me!'

Disappointed, Little Tiger cowered among the leaves.

Just a few days later, however, Mother decided it was finally time to let them out. That morning, Little Tiger's heart was racing.

Finally, she would see! Finally, she would know!

They lined up. First Mother, then her little brother and, lastly, her.

'Do not stray away from my tail!' Mother roared before leaving the den.

And so they left.

The sun shone high in the sky, so bright that the cubs' eyes were almost hurting. They advanced cautiously, squinting.

It was a beautiful spring day; new leaves were sprouting on the highest tree branches, and at the bottom of the trunks the first flowers were just beginning to bloom. The ground beneath their paws was soft and wet. The birds were singing above their heads, while other, smaller animals scampered off as soon as they saw them.

Then suddenly they heard a scary noise, far away at first, then closer and closer. The two cubs stopped, uncertain, with their tails straight and their whiskers and noses tensed, to try to understand the sound.

'It's the river,' Mother told them, turning. 'Soon you will see it too.'

And, indeed, a vast expanse of shimmering water soon appeared before their eyes. Large tree trunks crashed against white, glossy sheets of ice, producing the noise that had so frightened them moments before.

'There should always be a river in your Kingdom,' Mother said. 'We tigers need to drink plenty of water. Remember that!'

While the cubs timidly approached the river to drink, Mother kept talking. 'As you can see, the river is made of water, but when the stars are in the sky longer than the sun, the water turns into a hard surface called ice. You can't drink the ice and it can be your enemy.'

'It's not afraid of us?' Tiger Cub asked.

'We can't eat it,' Mother replied calmly.

'But it can't eat us either!'

'It can eat you even if it has no mouth. If you walk over it and it breaks, it'll drag you under. Then, if no trunks float by to cling to, it's very hard to get out of its grip.'

CHAPTER TWO

Lessons in Survival

The day after their first outing, Mother brought the pair of cubs a hare to eat in the den.

'You will start by hunting these,' she said as they were feasting on their first meat. 'After that you will move on to foxes, deer and then even larger creatures.'

The change of diet made them stronger and more confident in their steps every day, and so they were able to start exploring beyond the boundaries of their home.

The river was a good place to go hunting.

'Everything that can walk will need to drink sooner or later,' Mother had explained to them. 'So just lie low and wait. Lunging and Surprise are the arts you must master.'

As they explored the riverbanks and the birch woods, Mother also taught them the diversity of smells. The smell of mouse, the smell of hare, of ermine, fox, badger and boar. Everything that could run had a smell, and everything that had a smell could be eaten.

She also taught them that time isn't always the same. There is the short time made of very long days, and the very long time when days become short. If the day is short, the night is long; and when the night is long, snow and ice fall over the world.

Snow changes everything.

It changes the way predators must hunt and track their prey and, as a result, changes the way they return to their dens too.

'Follow the tracks, but never leave any – this is the secret of our kin. When a tiger moves, nobody should be able to work out their direction. It's easy when there's no snow, but the presence of snow makes things harder. Nobody should ever find out where your den is.'

'Why?' Tiger Cub asked.

'Because your den is where you will keep the most precious thing.'

'What?' Little Tiger persisted.

'Yourselves,' Mother replied, nuzzling them both.

'If we're Kings and Queens, what should we be afraid of?' Little Tiger wanted to ask, but the question got stuck at the back of her throat.

It was on a snowy day that they explored their first field. Mother hid behind a large trunk and sent them both off into the taiga to hunt. Little Tiger was better at it than her brother and soon reappeared with a rabbit in her mouth. It had been easy and fun, and the flesh seemed tastier than that of the hare Mother had brought them.

In the days that followed, Mother began to wander off, leaving them alone in the den.

'Do not go outside!' was her strict order every time.

She would stay away for one, two or even three days.

In the boredom of confinement, Little Tiger wondered about her mother's warning. Why weren't they supposed to go outside? If they really were Kings and Queens, what on Earth did they have to fear? They had already met the enemy that was Ice. Were there others too, perhaps?

Sometimes Tiger Cub wanted to play inside the den, but she didn't feel like it. She had seen the Outside, and now felt nostalgic for everything that happened in the sun.

Mother's return was always a cause for celebration. She would peer inside the den with her jaws clamped around a very big catch, which they would then drag down to the river together.

The first time, both cubs were in awe of such large prey. A hare or a mouse was easy to eat, but that huge buck? Where were they supposed to begin?

Mother gently nudged them towards the hind legs. 'Start from there, then keep eating until you feel full.'

The three of them ate in silence, side by side, for quite a long time. Every now and then they would peel themselves away from the carcass to go to drink from the river.

Some crows cawed loudly from the surrounding trees.

'Why do they do that?' Little Tiger asked, looking up at them.

'Because they're hungry.'

'When will they eat?'

'When we allow them to.'

Some of the smaller prey could be devoured in the time between sunrise and sunset, while others – moose or big deer – weren't stripped clean even by the time darkness fell. Then Mother and cubs would cover the carcass with branches and leaves and, instead of returning to the den, they would lie there, watching their meal closely. They soon learned that the crows were not the only creatures in the taiga that fed at the expense of others.

One sunny day, while they were devouring what remained of a moose, a male tiger appeared in the clearing. All three of them raised their muzzles from the carcass. Instead of leaping at his throat, Mother walked over to greet him, tail straight, and brushed her nose against his.

'Say hello to your father,' she told the cubs.

A little intimidated, Little Tiger and Tiger Cub ran over to rub their faces against his.

Their father stayed with them for three days, until not even a shred of meat was left on the moose carcass. At night they lay next to each other, lazily flicking their tails, engrossed in the sounds of the Great Forest breathing.

Father got up at the crack of dawn on the fourth day.

Eyes blazing, he told them: 'Remember! As long as you are true tigers, you will have the world at your feet. But if you allow another Spirit to possess you even for one moment, the world will notice and will turn you into a laughing stock.'

Whose Spirit? Little Tiger wanted to ask, and what is a laughing stock? But she didn't have a chance because Father rubbed his muzzle against theirs and then vanished into the silence of the taiga as suddenly as he had appeared.

CHAPTER THREE

A Voice Will Call You

Little Tiger and Tiger Cub were growing up fast.

They were not yet as large as their mother, but they no longer looked like cubs either. When all three were asleep in the den, between all the legs and tails there was hardly any room left.

They had continued their training throughout the long winter in the taiga. They had learned to walk on any terrain without making noise. Be it ice, mud or a carpet of leaves and branches, every step was to be shrouded in the deepest silence. They had learned to smell the air and read all of its messages. They had learned to listen to the wind and recognize its invisible words.

They had learned how to leap.

'Leap further and with more power!' Mother repeated relentlessly. 'Sneak up behind, jump on the back of your prey and go for the throat in one smooth and continuous movement.'

Such was the hard work of a tiger.

One evening, as they were returning to the den, Little Tiger, shaking the snow off her thick fur, asked her mother:

'How long will I be little for? My tail is almost as long as yours now.'

Mother smiled as only a tiger can – from the bottom of her heart. Many seasons earlier, she had asked the same question of her own mother.

'You will be little for as long as you stay with me.'

'And how long will we stay?' Tiger Cub asked.

'Until the day the taiga calls you.'

'But we are already in the taiga!' Little Tiger said.

'But the Kingdom where you live is mine. One day you will leave to conquer your own.'

'I'm happy here!' Little Tiger said.

'A day will come when that will no longer be true.'

'When will that be?'

'One morning, a voice will call you.'

'And then?'

'Then you will start running. And you will keep running and never turn back.'

'Won't we see each other again?' Tiger Cub asked.

'Enough now. Be quiet!' Mother said, resting her head on her front paws as her eyes closed wearily.

'We will meet again in the Taiga beyond the Sky,' she whispered, before drifting off to sleep.

One summer had already passed and another was almost over, when Little Tiger realized that life was not as simple as it had seemed during her first forays out of the den.

There were practical difficulties: walking on ice, finding prey. But there were also all kinds of other difficulties that were much harder to define.

Father's parting words kept echoing in her mind, but she had no answers.

Would she be a true tiger, or something else?

And what else?

A wild boar, a deer, a wolf, a crow?

What would she risk turning into if she were unable to become a true tiger?

'Always be true!' Mother kept repeating.

One night, in the warmth of the den, Little Tiger asked her what it meant to be 'true'.

'A tiger must be fully tiger,' she replied.

Then they had slept, side by side. Or rather, Mother had slept while Little Tiger remained awake, wide-eyed in the darkness of the den. She had seen old trees in the forest: their trunks were full of cracks, with mushrooms growing inside the deep cavities. Were they still trees, or were they fungus-trees?

Could such a thing happen to her too? At some point, if the integrity of her fur were breached and an opening created, would another nature be allowed to enter? Or would her own nature simply flow out?

Where would it go to?

How could she possibly know?

And how could somebody else's nature take over her? If she wasn't true, then some day would she turn into a rat or a hare? Instead of hunting, would she be hunted? Is there a difference between how things appear and how things really are? she wondered.

As the dawn light began creeping into the den, Little Tiger thought she had got only one thing clear in her mind: life truly was full of mysteries!

Over time, her mother began to notice that Little Tiger's hunting skills were not as promising as they had been in the beginning. While Tiger Cub lunged without hesitation, Little Tiger would often get distracted midway through the motion. Her body was present but her mind was not, and in that split second her prey was able to get enough speed to escape, and she lost it.

'What's the matter?' Mother asked her after a few resounding failures, but Little Tiger was unable to respond.

She should have said she was thinking, but tigers do not know what thinking means. Then Mother reminded her that nobody would ever be able to hunt in her place. Some day soon, her own survival and that of her cubs would depend entirely on the power of her legs.

Little Tiger nodded.

Yes, she understood.

Mother closed her eyes for a moment. That little one, of whom she had been so proud, now worried her. If she went on like that, what would become of her? As she watched her walk away against the blinding white of the snow, her tail swaying rhythmically with each step, Mother lowered her eyelids and prayed to the most powerful Spirits of the taiga.

'May the temptation of the Fox and the Crow always stay away from her,' she asked with the profound strength of her love.

'And may she never encounter mankind...'

CHAPTER FOUR

I Must Tell You about Mankind

The cubs' second winter was almost over. The ice sheets on the river were beginning to crack, while the snow on the ground was turning into a huge swamp. The sound of water dripping echoed all around. The birds had given up their gloomy winter peeping and were now chirping and warbling, hopping from branch to branch.

Soon it would be time for the brief mating season, and Mother knew that her cubs would leave to conquer their own Kingdoms.

How many times had she lived through that moment!

And every time her heart was still filled with pride for being able to carry out her task. But this feeling often overlapped with another feeling – one that was subtler and more mysterious, and that suddenly made her feel fragile.

As she rested in front of the entrance to the den,

she wondered if everything she had taught her cubs would be enough. Had she been clear enough? Strict enough? Would they be able to become true tigers?

Little Tiger and Tiger Cub were now old enough to hunt by themselves and spend the night outside. They often returned with some food for their mother as well. Tiger Cub was a specialist in boars. Little Tiger, however, favoured hares.

Mother had tried to reproach her, asking, 'Is that all?'

But her daughter always found an excuse: 'I wasn't hungry!...I ate a salmon!...I fell asleep in a clearing full of blueberries...'

Little Tiger had a curious nature, and curiosity was not a good virtue for a Queen. For squirrels, perhaps, but not for a tiger. A tiger should be able to go straight for her goal.

Mother sighed. She couldn't keep quiet any more. She had told them about everything except mankind.

Now it was time.

The thaw was already under way. Swarms of annoying insects rose from the huge wetlands the taiga had become. Tiger Cub had brought an old deer back to their den, and they spent two days doing nothing other than eating. It took just as long for them to digest it.

On the fourth day, Mother stood up and said, 'I must tell you about mankind!'

Tiger Cub opened his eyes sleepily. 'Can you eat it?'

'We could, but that's not the most important point.'

'So why must you tell us about it?'

'Because it is better that tigers and mankind do not meet, ever.'

Then Mother told them everything she knew. Out of all the animals, man was the only one able to put an end to their days. It was not very large, nor did it have nails or teeth worthy of those names. What he had, though, was a long rod out of which came fire, and with it he could kill tigers.

'Does he want to eat us?' Little Tiger asked.

Mother shook her head. 'No, the man kills just for the sake of killing.'

'In addition to the fire,' Mother went on, 'the man also knows how to build traps from which, once caught, it is very difficult to escape.'

'We've never seen one!' Little Tiger protested.

'Luckily there are very few of them,' Mother replied, 'but it is best to know how to recognize those few.'

Then she got up, inviting the cubs to follow.

'You need to know his smell. Learn to recognize it in even the most confusing winds, and whenever you sense it, you must flee in the opposite direction right away. Man also makes a lot of noise, especially if he's not alone, but if you ever get to hear that noise it will already be too late to do anything.'

'We tigers flee?' Tiger Cub exclaimed, surprised.

'What's the point in dying at the hands of someone who won't even eat you?' Mother sighed. 'A tiger respects the dignity of life.'

They walked in silence for a couple of days. Most of the time they followed the course of the river, then they headed into a vast forest of firs.

At one point, Mother stopped, sniffing the air. Then she started walking again, more cautiously now, in the same direction.

After a while, they found themselves at the edge of a clearing. A building made of wooden planks stood out in the middle. Part of the roof had collapsed and the area around it was neglected and overgrown.

'See, this is a man's den,' Mother whispered. 'An abandoned one.'

She was the first to approach it, with great caution, followed by her cubs.

Tiger Cub stopped, distracted by a pair of old boots. He moved forward nose first, sniffing all around.

'That's his smell?'

Mother nodded.

They entered the cabin and Mother urged them to sniff every little thing.

'Can you feel it? Can you? Do you understand?'

They explored every nook and cranny.

'I think there was more than one man here,' Tiger Cub remarked at one point.

'Right! This was a woodcutter's hut. At least four of them have been here.'

'Are they coming back?' Little Tiger asked.

'Not here,' Mother replied. 'They move around to cut trees.'

On the way back, the cubs were quiet, each absorbed in their own thoughts.

Now they knew that something else apart from the ice was a threat to them – and in the same way as the ice. Both would harm tigers not in order to survive, but only for the sake of doing so.

That year, the warm season was shorter than usual. The night devoured the daylight and they spent more and more time away from the den.

Mother knew that her cubs were fully grown. Soon she would be alone again, and then, if it so pleased the sky, a new life cycle would start.

For the first time since she had learned of her purpose as a tiger, she felt a vague sense of bewilderment. How many seasons had passed since her first litter? Closing her eyes, Mother tried to imagine how much of the taiga would be covered by her own Kingdom and the Kingdoms of her offspring. Her cubs must surely have ventured as far as where the sun rises. She could be proud. She had been a good mother; she had chosen a good father. It was he who brought her news of their offspring from time to time, as he was used to exploring much larger territories than hers.

In her heart, Mother smiled. Thinking about her children, and her children's children, she realized that it was possible that there was no corner of the vast forest that wasn't ruled by their progeny. Her life hadn't been very different from that of the large trees of the forest, after all. She had been the trunk, and her children the branches, and her children's children the fruit. But instead of embracing the sky with foliage, they reigned the entire Earth with their presence, bringing order to the world. No sick animal suffered and no creature lived longer than the forces of the sky allowed them to.

If it were not for man, the world would be perfect.

So many distant memories were now coming back to her. All of a sudden, she remembered the smouldering eyes of the one who had taught her that great truth years before: mankind is the principle of disharmony. Looking back on that time long ago, Mother let out a deep sigh.

CHAPTER FIVE

The Man-Tiger

Mother had been hardly bigger than Little Tiger when she met him. She had only just marked the boundaries of her Kingdom and was looking for the one who would become the father of her children. The snow had been falling for several days but the river was not yet completely frozen.

A young male of incredible magnificence had appeared at her side. They had sniffed each other, liked one another, and had begun chasing each other, jumping in the snow and wrapping their long tails around one another. Both were young and they had the same boundless energy, the same desire to be masters of the world.

It will be with him that I start my progeny, she had thought then, as they were catching their breath in between games. *Yes, he'll be the father of my children.*

At this thought she had felt a great peace settle

inside her. Everything had been accomplished. She had her Kingdom, and soon the cubs would come too.

But days passed and nothing happened between them except the pleasure of being together. They continued to play in the den as siblings, but that was all.

One day, as they recovered from one of their chasing games, their breath forming small puffy clouds in front of them, the young male had inhaled deeply, staring at her.

'There's something I have to tell you.'

It was time! Her heart had leapt.

'I would spend my whole life with you in the taiga, but I can't,' he said.

'Why not?'

'Because I am not a tiger, but a man.'

The Young Tiger had jumped up.

How could that be possible?

He looked exactly like one of her kin. Not even his smell had alerted her! They both stood still, staring at each other.

'I am a shaman, and the Tiger is my Spirit Guide. I live inside him, but I'm not him. Before the new moon, I'll go back to living as a human being, just as I was when I was born from my mother's womb.'

At those words, the Young Tiger had felt very

confused. She didn't know what a shaman was, but she knew that men were a great danger. She should have run away, but something compelled her to stay.

'Fear not!' he had told her, to put her mind at ease. 'My time is not up yet. We can stay together for two days more.'

And so they did.

But something had changed between them.

The Young Tiger had no longer felt like playing, so they had started talking. With Man-Tiger next to her, she could see things that had been invisible to her up until that point.

It was the Shaman who explained to her the reason why humans killed tigers without eating them. It was because they loved putting their skin under their feet. Once dead, in fact, a tiger was turned into a rug, while its entrails were used to create medications with which humans entertained the delusion that they could acquire its powers.

But the true reason why men liked to kill tigers wasn't even that, he had continued.

The real reason was envy.

They envied their strength and their majesty.

One snowy night, the Man-Tiger had shown her how perfect each snowflake looked just before melting on their fur. Together they had counted the stars, and they had kept vigil, waiting for the sun that would rise each day to start the world anew.

When the night of their parting finally came, they rubbed their muzzles together for a long time.

'All of this is very sad,' the Young Tiger had said.

'Everything has a meaning,' the Man-Tiger had replied, as he walked away from her slowly, vanishing into the fog that had engulfed the forest in the meantime.

After being buried in her memory for so many years, the words of the Shaman-Tiger were coming back to her now. Her survival instincts had almost led Mother to erase the memory of that episode.

And yet now, as she watched Little Tiger, she started to realize how different she was from all the other children she had borne, and how this difference could be a result of what she herself had learned during those nights long ago.

The Shaman had shown her a world that was invisible to others, and that world, trapped for so long inside her heart, had somehow found a way to surface in her offspring.

Without realizing it, the thoughts of Man-Tiger had become her thoughts, and her thoughts had become those of Little Tiger. She, however, had managed to dominate them, while Little Tiger was dominated by them.

CHAPTER SIX

What Will Become of Her?

At night, in the den, Mother watched her daughter sleep. She was an adult tiger now and she would have been the pride and joy of any mother. She slept with a serene expression, her stomach vibrating with each breath and her whiskers following the same rhythm.

She should have been ready by now to conquer her own Kingdom and find a mate, yet every time her mother looked at her she couldn't help but see anything more than a rug.

The last three days they spent together were disrupted by an enormous snowstorm. In the dim light of the den they could hear the wind whistling, accompanied by the sudden crash of the older trees collapsing to the ground and the subsequent crackling of branches.

'The wind speaks,' Mother told her cubs repeatedly. 'You just need to know how to listen.'

Little Tiger couldn't sleep. The wind was speaking with the energy of a storm but, try as she might, she couldn't decipher a single word.

Her brother was restless too, pacing back and forth in the den as if his tail were on fire.

'When will it end?' he asked over and over again.

'When it pleases the sky,' Mother answered patiently.

Tiger Cub felt a surge of anger.

'The sky – always the sky! There must be something that depends on our legs!'

That first rebellious outburst made it clear to Mother that the time for farewells had come. Once the storm had subsided, their family would part.

'Yes, what about our legs?' Little Tiger joined in. 'If we are destined to reign, why must we submit to something else?'

'The sky is our father,' came Mother's calm reply. 'The Earth our mother. Our Kingdom is what comes in between. If the father wants something, it's for our own good. Likewise, if the mother wants it. A wise tiger knows how to listen.'

But Mother's words didn't placate the restless young tigers.

Tiger Cub kept moving over to the entrance of the den, pawing vigorously at the wall of snow that was accumulating there, repeating: 'We're not rats!'

Then one day, just before dawn, the wind suddenly subsided.

The silence that follows a storm is the greatest silence of all. Everything is still, and the blanket of snow sparkles in the light of the sun. With gentle thuds, the branches of the fir trees are released from their white burden and the birds, baffled, keep repeating a single note. More than a song, it sounds like a question: '*Chirp?* Is it really over? *Chirp?* Really? Is it over?'

When the first rays of the sun entered the den, Mother knew that the moment for which she had been waiting for so long had finally arrived. That day, her children would begin their solitary adult lives. They would rub their long muzzles against hers and then their tails would slowly disappear from her sight in opposite directions.

During those stormy days, however, looking back at the many times Little Tiger had returned happily to the den, shaking just a hare in her mouth as proudly as a fox would, Mother had made a decision.

What kind of a Kingdom could her daughter ever hope to find for herself?

Heading out into the thick snow, Mother turned back towards her children.

'The Big Moment has arrived! But it's not nice to part ways like this. I will go out hunting for you one last time! I'll bring back a moose more succulent than you've ever eaten. Then we will feast and you will be on your way.'

'Yes!' Little Tiger and Tiger Cub answered in unison, lifting their muzzles high in a salute.

As soon as Mother was out of sight, they threw themselves on to each other one last time, chasing each other in a childish game of rough and tumble.

Mother had a hard time making her way through all the snow. As soon as she reached the top of the hill overlooking the entrance to their den, she turned around one last time to look at her children. Little Tiger was crouching and hissing from the bottom of her lungs, and Tiger Cub was pretending to be scared. In a moment, she knew, he'd jump over her and they would both roll joyfully in the snow.

She had made the right decision.

Inheriting a Kingdom was easier than conquering one. If someone were to become a rug, it had better be her, not Little Tiger.

She closed her eyes, opened them, closed them once more, and then opened them one last time. She wanted that scene to remain forever imprinted in her heart.

'May the sky protect you, and the Earth be your friend,' she whispered.

Then, with a giant leap, she disappeared among the immense white silhouettes of trees covered with snow.

CHAPTER SEVEN

To the East

Little Tiger and Tiger Cub waited for their mother for six days, hunting small prey from time to time to feed themselves.

They waited in vain.

On the seventh day, waking up his sister, Tiger Cub said, 'She's not coming back.'

Little Tiger was alarmed. 'Why do you say that?'

'It doesn't take seven days to catch a moose.'

'Let's wait a bit longer.'

'You wait! I must go.'

'Where are you going?'

'To where the sun goes down.'

As they said goodbye, their noses brushed one last time.

'You've been a good sister.'

'And you a good brother.'

'Goodbye.'

'Goodbye.'

After a few uncertain steps, the young male sped up his gait and walked away without looking back.

It had been snowing steadily since the day of the storm. The area around the clearing was beaten by their paw prints.

Uncertain, Little Tiger stood in front of the entrance to the den.

The silence was broken only by the crackling noise of a squirrel gnawing at a pine cone overhead.

It was the first time that Little Tiger had been completely alone.

Alone in front of the den, alone inside the den.

The flattened leaves on the ground still smelled of her mother and brother.

It was only when night fell that she reluctantly stepped inside. There was nobody to keep her warm, nobody to curl up against. Lonely sleep was the saddest of all, and the lightest too. At every rustling noise she leaped to her feet, heart pounding, expecting an attack. She would then push her muzzle through the tangle of branches, but the cold moonlight on the snow always illuminated the same sight: black skeletons of trees against a black sky.

No creatures, no movement.

Why wasn't Mother coming back?

Little Tiger couldn't understand.

She waited one more week, hunting hare to eat. Then, after yet another sleepless night, she decided that since Mother had not returned, she would go after her. Perhaps she had fallen into a trap, or maybe she was hurt and needed her help.

She couldn't wait any longer.

So she started walking in the opposite direction to her brother. If he had gone where the sun sets then she would go to the East, where it rises. Invigorated by this decision, she crossed the river, springing nimbly from trunk to trunk, and then ventured into the Great Forest.

After walking for several days, however, Little Tiger stopped. Eight times the sun had risen, and eight times it had disappeared, swallowed up by the darkness of the night. Although she had kept up a good pace, that magnificent red disc had not got closer. How could that be possible? If she followed a hare or a fox, at some point the distance shortened, until it disappeared.

Why is the sun immune to this law?

Little Tiger kept on walking, trying to unlock this secret, but she could feel the mystery flying further out of reach – just like when she was a cub and she tried pouncing on the pheasants feeding in the glades. Too much clumsiness, too much hassle, and all she was left with were a few feathers between her paws. The solar disc behaved in exactly the same way. The more she chased it, the more it eluded her.

Was it the only thing that eluded her?

Didn't she feel the same sense of bewilderment towards the snowflakes that rested on her fur? For a moment, there was absolute perfection before her eyes. What seemed to be just a dot floating in the air turned into a tiny perfect star when it reached her paw, barely lasting the time it took her to blink.

And so?

What was the mystery hidden behind the impermanence of perfection?

Although she was failing to reach the sun, Little Tiger didn't want to give up. She had to get to the edge of their Kingdom, at all costs.

'We will meet again in the Taiga beyond the Sky,' Mother had said, a few days before disappearing.

And where on Earth could such a Kingdom start if not in the exact spot where each day begins?

Snowstorms raged and then subsided. The birches and maple trees put on their leaves, only to lose them again. The undergrowth filled up with berries; the air with swarms of insects. The ground became a quagmire; the quagmire became ice and was, in turn, covered by snow. The birds migrated, leaving the sky silent and empty. The trees became naked again, and Tiger, who was no longer little, pushed on towards the East, chasing the sun that continued to elude her.

One morning, the Tiger woke up and felt a sort of emptiness in her stomach. It wasn't hunger, because she had devoured a young boar the night before. It was something different. For two years now, she had walked alone, and that journey was beginning to take its toll. Her mother, her brother and the carefree life of the den were nothing but faded memories.

Ahead of her, there was only nothing.

Was that the purpose of her life?

She knew that she would have to build a Kingdom for herself, but she had no idea how and, most importantly of all, to what avail.

Perhaps that was the reason for the void she felt in her stomach: that she was no longer able to understand the purpose of her actions.

Surely she needed to meet the father of her children, breed cubs and raise them, release them into the world and breed others, like her mother had done, and her mother's mother, and her mother's mother's mother? That way her Kingdom would stretch to the edges of the taiga, reaching the sun, the moon, and even the border between the sun and the moon.

Repeating what others have done.

Was this really the meaning of life?

'The sky sets a destiny for everyone,' Mother had told her.

'A tiger must always be a tiger!' Father had growled.

What did they mean?

'You must not let any other nature in,' had been her father's warning.

'The thoughts of the Fox shall not be your thoughts. The eyes of the Crow shall not be your eyes,' her mother had urged.

Now, as she walked wearily across the taiga, the Tiger could not forget the fiery look in her father's eyes. What would he say if he saw her wandering so aimlessly? He would be disappointed – very disappointed. Maybe he would tell her she was only fit to become a rug.

Was it really so?

During the previous season, she had caught the scent of a male on a birch trunk. She had left her own scent in turn, but nothing had happened. Was it her fault? Or was it Fate that compelled her to be a tiger that was not a true tiger?

And if her destiny was not that of a tiger, what could it be?

The Tiger felt a great emptiness inside her.

That void was nothing more than a well, a gaping chasm between her mind and heart. It was

a hollow that swallowed her attention and it was from there, from that unfathomable depth, that all of the questions surfaced.

At first, the Tiger thought that being patient would be enough. Just by waiting there, sitting on the edge, she would find the answers sooner or later.

But all that came from the bottom of the well was a slight dripping of water. Darkness was darkness, and remained so even if she leaned inside and roared with all the strength in her body. All she got back was the echo of her own voice.

Raaaaawwr...rrrr...rrrr...

The Tiger felt lonely.

Another form of nature had crept up inside her, like the fungi on the trees.

What form of nature was it?

Where did it come from?

Of one thing, at least, the Tiger was certain: instead of choosing, she had been chosen.

But by whom?

Why?

And when?

All of these questions kept echoing back and forth, pointless and silent, between the walls of the well.

CHAPTER EIGHT

The Tiger of Nothing

Days and months passed. Months turned into years.

The Tiger had walked for so long that the leaves on the trees had changed many times and generations of cubs of all kinds had begun to scurry out of their dens and shelters.

She had fed herself, yes, but absentmindedly. She ate only the small prey that ended up beneath her paws. She was not at all like her mother, who hunted fiercely. Feeding the children or merely staying alive – that was the difference between them.

In this way, still moving towards the East, the Tiger had become the Queen of Nothing. She had claimed no territory, experienced no encounters that might lead to any sort of future. Her skin seemed to be hanging off her bones, her eyes marked by the volatile uncertainty of her days.

Leaving the beaten track for an unfamiliar path contained within itself the seed of madness. She knew that this had always been the rule.

But what if it wasn't enough for her?

What if she couldn't settle?

Dreadful is the loneliness of those tigers who have chosen the path of the wanderer. Here today, gone tomorrow, chasing shadows and dreams, chasing the nagging thought that is forever whispering: *Keep going, this is not the place yet.*

But keep going where?

And why?

From time to time, feeling desperate from too much loneliness, she even tried to talk to other species of animals.

'Come closer. Eat with me,' she said to a fox who had walked by the clearing while she was eating, but the fox, certain that he would only end up being the final titbit of her meal, walked away with the light steps of his kind.

Her second attempt was with a bear, a she-bear who had emerged from the den with her younglings to enjoy the first summer sun. Seeing her arrive, the bear stood up on her hind legs in all her fierceness, slashing the air with her clawed paws.

'Come on, if you want to fight! I'm ready!' she challenged her.

The Tiger remained still for a while, undecided.

Would she be able to make the bear understand that all she wanted was a little company?

No, she would not. So she turned around slowly, leaving the menacing bear to defend her den.

Being the terror of everyone while not wanting to be the terror of anyone: such was her curse. Denying her own nature to reach out to a new one, which was as yet unknown to her; wandering around in complete loneliness, wishing for nothing but the comfort of company.

During the fourth year of uninterrupted wandering, the Tiger realized there wasn't much of a difference between a tiger without a Kingdom and a rug.

She didn't want to be what others expected her to be, and a great weariness fell upon her. She had given up their Kingdom in the taiga to find another one, but in this she had failed.

She had spent many seasons travelling towards the East, convinced that, eventually, the sun would reveal the secret of its light to her. But years had passed, and the distance remained the same. The sun rose, the sun set, and her initial joyful energy had slowly and inexorably turned into deadly exhaustion.

What kind of future lay ahead of her?

To keep going around in circles between sunrise and sunset? To drag her feet along a path that no longer held any surprises? The monotonous hunting of small prey to ensure her survival?

What had this long journey of hers been, then?

Maybe it really would be better to be turned into a rug.

Maybe it was because of such thoughts, or maybe because Fate had already mapped out her path, but at some point, the thing that Mother had always feared ended up happening.

It all happened rather accidentally.

In the hushed silence of the winter forest, the Tiger suddenly heard the crunching of snow. She realized right away that no paw could make that noise.

Who could it be, then, if not a human being?

And yet there were no villages or roads nearby.

With cautious steps, her belly brushing the ground as she crouched down low, she moved in the direction of the noise, and after a while she saw them among the pine trees.

There were indeed two men – the first ones she had ever seen!

They did not look particularly threatening as they made their way through the snow, walking on strange feet similar to those of the ducks. She could also hear their voices. They were arguing, as if they were anxious about something. One of them had a gun, but they did not look like hunters.

Not even a child would venture into the taiga without a weapon. They had no dogs with them, which was a good thing.

Crawling on her stomach and keeping downwind, the Tiger began to follow them.

Where were they going?

She really couldn't work it out.

And so, before the sky turned dark, she arrived at the hut. It was in the middle of a clearing. Two wooden logs, that reminded her of men's legs, rested under the roof next to a pile of logs. A plume of smoke was coming out of the chimney and a light was shining behind the glass.

Someone did live there, after all. She had never noticed that before, although she had passed by the hut several times already.

It was there that the two men were heading. The Tiger saw them shake the snow from their felt boots and timidly knock on the door, waiting.

When the door finally opened, the night was already descending on the taiga. The two visitors bowed to the silhouette of a man, who bowed back, before they were each swallowed by the wooden wall.

This meeting unsettled the Tiger.

Who could live in that house? Certainly not a hunter. In all the time she had circled around that area, she had never heard the echo of a shot, even from afar.

So who was it, then?

Humans usually take comfort from living next

to each other, Mother had told her. If they leave the village for the forest it is only because they have a task to accomplish: procuring food or skins, picking mushrooms, gathering berries. Once their task has been completed, they immediately return to their kin.

Why had those men come here? From the purposefulness in their steps, it was clear that they weren't lost – they knew exactly where they were going. And if they knew, there had to be a reason.

A reason they knew, but that the Tiger could not figure out.

The next day, a snowstorm began and erased any trace of the men's passage.

The Tiger was still crouching, waiting not far from them. In the raging storm, only the tips of her ears and tail were sticking out.

The door of the hut had never been opened; the fire inside had never gone out. There was no noise to be heard aside from the wind that howled through the trees, furiously sweeping the snow from the branches that bent gently and elegantly, creaking and sometimes crashing.

As the third sunset dawned, the storm began to subside.

By the middle of the night, the clouds had dissolved and the moon was shimmering, suspended above the pine trees, surrounded by a magnificent parade of stars that were reflected on the sparkling snow blanket.

The Tiger shook the snow from her fur. She had lived through so many storms already. And when each one came to an end, she could not help but wonder at the enchanted harmony they left behind.

Was this one of life's rules perhaps?

Under the brutal lashing of the elements, reality becomes blurred: it seems there is no longer any order and everything is irretrievably lost. Then, suddenly, everything comes together and order is restored in the world, along with a sense of awe at the beauty and balance that permeates all things.

The Tiger moved closer to the hut and began to wait, sheltered by the thick snow.

She did not know what she was waiting for – she just knew that she was breaking the Great Law, which states that tigers and men should be masters of territories very distant from each other. There was no hope of survival for the human being who dared to cross the threshold of the Kingdom of a tiger. The same could be said for a tiger who, either by mistake or folly, trespassed into the territory of men.

She knew she was disobeying her mother's teaching. The very teaching that was handed down from generation to generation.

Danger, danger, danger! said every fibre of her body, from her whiskers to the very tip of her tail.

'Remember: you get close to the man only to devour him. If you let him act first, the risks you take are unpredictable and incalculable.'

'What risks?' she had asked.

'The rifle. The rifle that draws blood, and the rifle that puts you to sleep. The leghold trap, the net that tangles you and turns you into a fish. You struggle, you try to free yourself, but there's no hope left for you.'

Why, then, did the Tiger decide to take such a big risk?

She did not know, but she knew she couldn't help it.

Soon after the dawn of the third day, the door opened and the two men left. With a bow they bid farewell to their host on the threshold. They put on their snowshoes and headed back the way they had come. They weren't chatting as they had been when they arrived; instead, they seemed lost in thought, silent.

For a moment, the Tiger was unsure what to do.

Should she follow them or stay close to the hut? Of course, if she followed them, sooner or later she would end up at a village – a risk she did not feel like taking.

The Man in the log cabin seemed more interesting. Who could he be, she wondered, to escape the company of other human beings? Someone like her, perhaps. Someone who had chosen – or who had been chosen – to open up to another dimension. Maybe he didn't even own a gun. Maybe he too had that unfathomable void inside him, only capable of generating questions.

Those long days spent watching the hut had taught the Tiger that she was more comfortable waiting than she was ambushing. She had no desire to tear or mangle, or to display any form of supremacy. The hunger that consumed her was, rather, for knowledge. So, alert, head erect, forelegs crossed, her long tail softly flicking across the surface of the snow, she began her wait to meet the Man.

CHAPTER NINE

I've Been Waiting for You

The snow continued to fall, covering the previous layer that hadn't yet melted. The deer were having a hard time digging through the thick blanket to find food in the soil. They raised their heads towards the branches, stretching their lips to nip at the lichens and using their horns to scrape the bark from the tender trunks of the birch trees.

The Tiger loved the winter more than the summer; the still silence of the snow more than the humming of myriad insects. Food was hard to come by, true, but filling her belly had never been her main concern. The white blanket that covered everything infused her with a kind of inner majesty. Wasting time chasing bloodsucking parasites belonged to a whole other dimension.

Despite this, she sometimes felt as though she were being tormented by hissing and humming noises, even in the dead of winter. It wasn't mosquitoes or horseflies, but the obsessive persistence of her own thoughts. They crept inside her head, where there was no door she could open and let them out. Crushing these thoughts beneath her paws or striking them with her tail was out of the question too. In spite of all her imposing strength, in such moments she felt helpless.

The Tiger spent weeks circling the hut discreetly, careful not to be seen or heard. She saw the Man emerge for short periods of time, carrying a basket to gather firewood.

She studied him.

He looked neither young nor old. Or, better yet, neither soft nor chewy, as Mother had described. Truth be told, she had seen more of his back than his face.

Once she thought she heard him singing.

If the Man had ventured further from the woodshed, he probably would have noticed that the snow around the hut had been trodden by the heavy paws of a tiger. What would he have done then? Would he have reached for his rifle?

Oddly enough, the Tiger wasn't afraid at all. She could attack first, of course, to defend herself, but that prospect left her completely indifferent. If she devoured him, the only thing she'd get out of it was a full belly for a few days. Then she would be back to square one.

Why was she spending so much time there?

She couldn't answer that.

Does a bee know why it's drawn to a flower? A mysterious power suddenly calls, impossible to resist. What might seem folly to one creature seems to another the only possible way forward.

One morning, as the ice on the highest branches was beginning to melt, the door of the hut opened and the Man came out to dig the snow that had piled up.

The Tiger didn't see him immediately – she was several leaps away – but she caught his scent very clearly. Cautiously, she retraced her steps, careful not to reveal her presence.

All she could hear was the cawing of a crow close by.

Suddenly, a voice echoed in the silence.

'I've been waiting for you.'

The Tiger stopped.

Where did that voice come from? She hesitated, her paw hovering in mid-air above the snow.

Run away?

Or move forward?

She moved forward.

When she was so close that she could feel the breath of the Man, she heard the voice again.

'Why are you hiding? I know you live next to me.'

At that, the Tiger gathered her courage and walked out into the open.

The Man had a shovel in his hand. They stared at each other for a long time, in silence. The only thing moving was the Tiger's tail.

'Remember,' Mother had once warned her, 'the gaze of the man and the tiger can never meet. We're not the ones who are afraid: it's men who flee in terror.'

How long did they remain like that, perfectly still?

'Take him out. Eat him so I can eat too,' the crow cawed impatiently up on the branch.

But the Tiger did not move.

The rays of the sun were touching the snow, making it sparkle with light.

Little clouds of steam were coming out of both their nostrils.

'Is it you I hear talking to me?' the Tiger asked, at last.

'Yes,' the Man replied.

'But men and tigers don't speak the same language.'

'They don't speak it if they don't want to. I inhale; you exhale. The whole universe breathes. For this reason, every voice is the same.'

Are you deceiving me, perhaps? the Tiger thought, but the Man seemed to read her mind.

'If I am here, it is precisely to avoid any deception.'

In the days that followed, the Tiger learned to approach the Man. He didn't call her, but she felt irresistibly drawn to him. She would follow him around as he was shovelling snow, fixing his skis or chopping firewood.

'Aren't you afraid that I might maim you?' she asked him the next day.

'If you'd wanted to eat me, you could have done it a thousand times already. Look up there,' he added with a smile, 'and see how disappointed that crow is.'

'You really feel no fear at all?' the Tiger roared softly.

The Man sighed. 'I have one particular fear, yes, and it's always the same. Not the fear of death but of not being able to be myself.'

That night, dozing off in front of the Man's door, the Tiger slept soundly – more so than she had in a long time. She was no longer alone. For mysterious reasons, someone else shared her fear.

'Are you a shaman?' she asked him one evening in the hut, while the wind hissed through the cracks between the logs.

The Man remained silent for a long time, and then, with a distant voice, he answered, 'My grandfather was one, and so was my father and my grandfather's father. I was supposed to be one as well.'

'So you're not, then?'

'No.'

'Then why do people come looking for you?'

'Because they think I am one.'

'You deceive them?'

'It is exactly because I don't deceive them that they leave empty-handed.'

'Empty-handed?'

'No amulets, no magic formula.'

'And they come back?'

The Man shook his head. 'They go to seek elsewhere what they do not find here.'

'What is it that they don't find?'

'A solution that will allow them not to change.'

The Tiger remained silent for a while. Then she said, 'You're not a hunter either, though.'

'No, I'm not. I hunt only what I need to feed myself.'

'Why don't you live in the village with the other men, then?'

In the twilight that was illuminated by the afterglow of the sunset, the Tiger saw the Man's face turn around to stare at her. The whites of his eyes gleamed in an extraordinary way.

'And you? Why do you not live like the other tigers?'

CHAPTER TEN

A Hand and Its Glove

Even though he wasn't a shaman, the Man was able to foretell what was going to happen. Whenever he sensed he was about to receive a visit, he would send the Tiger out into the forest. It was better if no one knew that a man and a tiger lived together, sharing their food and their thoughts. Once he was alone again, all he had to do was say 'Come back', and the Tiger would return solemnly to the hut.

They also went hunting together.

'Something wants us to put an end to its days,' he would occasionally say, getting to his feet.

He would take his rifle and together they would head off to meet the animal that had sought him out. The Man was, in fact, able to talk to all living creatures, just as he did with her.

'There is an appreciation for life,' the Man had explained, 'just as there is a gratitude for death. The two things are intertwined, like a tree and the vine that engulfs it.'

The Tiger had never thought about death, perhaps because she had not yet seen one of her kin lying lifeless. The only death she knew was the one that she regularly bestowed upon other living creatures.

'I've never thought about it,' she said that night, by the fire.

'The fear of death is a privilege reserved for humans.'

'Why are they afraid?'

'Because they leave behind the known for the unknown.'

'Even the tigers?'

'Even the tigers, of course.'

'But tigers are not afraid.'

'They're not afraid because they are unable to imagine the future.'

'Is that the only reason?'

'No. It is also because they are not forced to choose.'

'Choose what?'

'Between doing good or evil.'

'Humans think we are evil. That's why they kill us.'

'You just act according to your nature. The evil that humans see in you is the evil that thrives in their hearts.'

'What about me, then?'

'What about you?'

'Why can't I live like the other tigers?'

'I cannot live like the other humans either.'

'Why?'

'Sometimes it just happens like this. Someone is born and they refuse to walk on the same path that others have trodden.'

The Tiger recalled the time her mother had taken her and her brother to the hut that the woodcutters had abandoned, encouraging them to sniff and learn the scent of anything that had been touched by the humans, teaching them to be wary of their cunning ways. Humans carried those long canes that shoot fire, and they could also craft devious traps.

'What's a trap?' Little Tiger had asked.

'A trap is something you can't see and that captures you when you least expect it.'

'Like a game?' asked Tiger Cub.

Mother had shaken her head gravely. 'It's not a game. For a tiger, a trap means certain death.'

She had then tried to explain to them what the traps she had seen looked like.

'You notice the trap only once you're already inside. That's why you should never let yourself get distracted; never look higher than ground level while you walk. Always sniff the air carefully and change course immediately if you catch the smell of humans from afar.'

In the early days she spent close to the Man, the Tiger often remembered the serious look in her mother's eyes as she told them those things. What if the friendly demeanour of that human was just a different kind of trap? That's why she had hesitated so much before crossing the threshold of his Hut. That apparent mellowness, that way he had of talking to her as if they were cubs from the same litter – couldn't those simply be a way to trick her?

But then, as the sun set after a frosty day, the Man had turned to look at her before entering the hut.

'Why don't you come inside? It would be nice to sleep next to each other. In exchange for your warmth I could tell you some stories.'

The Tiger had stared at him for a long time, shaking her head to get rid of the ice on her fur.

Nearby, some crows cawed loudly.

'You don't trust me?'

The Tiger didn't answer.

'You think I only want your fur instead of your company?'

'That's right.'

'But I trusted *you*. You might have wanted only my blood and my flesh instead of my company.'

'I've never thought about your blood and your flesh.'

'Nor have I ever thought about your fur.'

The Man had remained on the threshold a while longer, holding the door open. The dim light of a small lamp shone at the back of the room. The sun had set; the creatures of the night had yet to start making their noises, while those that belonged to the day were already quiet. The only sound was the crackling of the fire in the stove.

'So?'

A thousand conflicting thoughts were swirling around in the Tiger's mind. Her head kept telling her that she still did not know enough about the countless tricks of humans, while her heart pushed her to go inside.

Eventually, she listened to her heart.

With slow steps and her tail raised halfway, she approached the door. As she stepped inside, she experienced for a brief moment what her prey must feel just before they meet their end. The pang of unadulterated dread.

Something terrible could have happened – something final.

Nothing did.

'Welcome!' the Man had said, pointing at a rug where she could lie down.

They spent a good part of their first winter together just like that: lying by the fire next to one another, talking.

The first story the Man told her was his own. Until then, other than considering them a possible meal or a potential danger, the Tiger had known nothing about humans and their ways – she had never even caught a glimpse of one of their cubs. Slowly, by listening to him, she came to know about their world. The more the Man spoke of himself, the more it seemed to the Tiger that he was talking about her too. Both had disappointed their parents; both had refused to become what tradition and nature expected them to become.

One evening, in a moment of silence, they heard a faint noise coming from the table next to them.

Skreech…skreech…skreech.

'Do you hear that?' asked the Man.

'What is it?'

'It's a woodworm. Such a small creature you can barely imagine it. It just hides in there and, slowly and patiently, it'll eat away the entire table. One day I will put down a plate and the whole thing will collapse into a heap of sawdust.'

'What kind of story is this?' asked the Tiger.

'A story that concerns us.'

'Can woodworms attack us?'

'Not our bodies, but our souls. You are a tiger with a woodworm inside you; I am a human with a woodworm inside me.'

'What makes you say that?'

'Because, just like me, you don't settle.'

'Settle? What does that mean?'

'Accepting things as they are, even if they are wrong – even if they lead to your death rather than life.'

'But you die anyway.'

'The soul can die long before the body.'

'So?'

'Those who have a woodworm inside them are always looking for another horizon.'

'Why?'

'Because they always sense another world beyond the one in which they live.'

The Tiger pondered this idea.

Hadn't that been precisely her own state of mind since the day she had left the den? She had never perceived any territory as her own. She had never stopped walking towards the East, towards the land where the sun rises. Why did she ever do that, if not because of the profound and unfathomable conviction that there was another world concealed beyond the horizon, and that, one way or another, that world had something to do with her?

'You don't know it yet, but you feel that you must know it,' said the Man. 'You sense a fire within you, and you don't know where the spark that generated it is hiding. Isn't that so?'

'It is...yes,' the Tiger admitted thoughtfully.

During that long winter, the Tiger and the Man got to know each other like no one else had before.

When the thawing snow began to drip from the roof, the Man said, 'Now we are just like a hand and its glove.'

The Tiger learned about all the invisible inhabitants of the taiga. There were goblins, ghosts and demons. The Man had learned all their stories from his father and grandfather. Both had been great shamans, moving between dimensions just as ordinary people walk through doors.

'I could call them with a whistle, and they would be at my feet in a flash,' he once confided to her.

'Then why don't you?'

'Because between freedom and power, I chose freedom.'

The Tiger was not yet able to fully understand his words, so, on an uneventful day, she begged him to cast one of those spells.

The Man uttered some unintelligible words and clapped his hands loudly three times.

Suddenly, a fearsome creature materialized right in front of them. It looked like some sort of ball, but it wasn't. At first it was an oval, then it became a rectangle. Unusually long and curly nails poked out from its body. Bristly silver hair that seemed never to have known a pair of scissors covered its face, wrapping around its body like a tangled web.

Above its tiny nose flashed a pair of eyes so narrow they looked like slits. The creature had no ears, and its mouth appeared to be frozen in an endless yawn.

The Tiger backed away warily.

'What is that?'

'The demon that was closest to us.'

'Who is that?'

'The demon of boredom.'

The Tiger looked more closely at the demon, noticing that its body exuded a kind of mist. The closer it got to her, the more she felt overpowered by a sort of irresistible drowsiness.

The Man clapped his hands three times and said some more mysterious words and, just like that, the demon vanished.

The Tiger felt better immediately.

'Remember that demons are like dogs: they love human company. You must always be very careful with demons. If you call them or let them get too close, there is a risk that they'll never go away.'

'Show me the opposite energy to that demon,' the Tiger said.

The Man took a tiny bell from his pocket and began to sing in a voice that the Tiger had never imagined he could have, alternating his song and the tinkling of the bell.

For a moment that seemed to the Tiger to last for ever, nothing happened.

Then, all of a sudden, a giant, luminous whirlwind that looked as if it contained all the colours and shades of the universe rolled in from the edge of the glade.

The Tiger braced herself to face the gusts of a tornado, but when it passed over their heads she realized the only strength inside it was that of a caress. The strange apparition emitted the most beautiful colours and scents in the world.

'What is this?' she asked the Man, as soon as the vortex had moved on.

'It's the energy that makes everything bloom, that makes the buds bulge and that, when the right season comes, turns them into flowers.'

CHAPTER ELEVEN

Wanderers in the Taiga

How long did the Tiger remain with the Man?

The snow melted, and buds and catkins started to appear on the bushes and trees. The great ritual of mating began, soon followed by the appearance of a new generation of creatures. When the youngsters were ready to leave their dens and nests, billions of insects descended upon the taiga. After the insects came the berries and, after the berries, the leaves turned yellow once more. Red, orange, golden yellow. At times, it seemed as if slivers of sun were falling to the ground.

Once again the snow returned, leaving the bare branches of the trees standing against the sky, like the hooked fingers of an old crone. The first flakes were followed by many others, and the landscape yet again resembled the one that had welcomed the Tiger the first time she came to the hut.

When the snow retreated from the glade, the visits of the humans were likely to become more frequent, so the Man and the Tiger dug a deep den in the dense forest, hidden behind the trunk of a large, dead tree. As soon as she sensed someone approaching, the Tiger would hide inside and fall asleep as she waited for the Man to call her back to the hut.

Whenever they were sure there were no humans around, the Man and the Tiger would wander across the taiga together. The Man always carried a leather shoulder bag and he collected berries and buds and tree bark as he walked, separating them from the fungi that he put in a small sack.

His tiger companion always attracted the attention of a large number of crows. Swarms of mosquitoes and insects fluttered around, tormenting the Man but never managing to penetrate the Tiger's long, thick fur.

Every now and then, the Tiger came home with some prey, though it was never particularly impressive. In those moments, she couldn't help recalling her father's disappointed expression as she returned from one of her first hunting forays with a hare still warm in her mouth.

'Are you a fox, then?' he had asked her, before vanishing into the forest without saying goodbye.

It was the foxes that caught mice, hares, partridges, pheasants: all the small creatures they could easily carry between their jaws. A tiger's prey was large, immovable, and a great many other inhabitants of the taiga could benefit from their death.

'That's why they call us Queens,' her mother had explained, that same evening in the den. 'They fear us and respect us. They fear us for our power; they respect us for our generosity. Many die because of us, but many more are able to survive thanks to us.'

During their hikes, the Man and the Tiger occasionally had fun chasing each other and romping among the trees like cubs, before collapsing together on the soft carpet of moss, exhausted. In those moments the Tiger felt that the Man became just like her in all respects.

They found ways to play even during the long winter months. With so little space to move inside the hut, the Man's challenge was to touch the Tiger's tail with the tip of his nose as it whipped through the air.

Sometimes, the Man went off to visit his kin and came back to the hut sad and pensive.

'Did they hurt you?' the Tiger would ask.

The Man would shake his head. 'No, but their pain got inside my heart.'

Many people with serious ailments would call

upon him, convinced that he would be able to help them. The most harrowing cases were those mothers who begged him to heal a sick child.

'There is nothing more terrible,' the Man had confided to her once.

The Tiger had nodded, remembering the expression of pained apprehension on her mother's face every time she and her brother wandered away from the den.

'There are pains that come from ourselves,' the Man went on, 'and others that come from the sky. The first are like knots in a tightrope. You have to be patient, to recognize the kind of knot it is and then have strong enough fingers to untangle it. As for the others, sadly, there is nothing you can do.'

'Nothing?' the Tiger repeated, amazed. Until that moment, she had thought there were no obstacles that the Man couldn't overcome.

'If a child dies, it dies. Not even the most advanced healing methods will be able to bring it back to life.'

'We're all going to die.'

'When our time comes, yes. But some die before their time, before they've taken their first steps, too early on their journey. And we find that hard to accept. The injustice of Fate. Some have a lot; some a little; others nothing at all. If I leave the hatch of the stove open with the fire burning while I'm out hunting and a piece of burning wood falls out, and on my return I find a pile of smouldering ash instead of my house, who's to blame?'

'You.'

'But if a storm breaks out while I'm wandering around the taiga and lightning strikes the house, and as I walk back I can already see the fire from afar, who's to blame?'

The Tiger pondered quietly, then said, 'The sky, which drops lightning where it should not.'

'That's right,' the Man agreed. 'But then, the real question becomes: can the sky wish us harm?'

The Tiger then thought about the sky, which she had so often looked up to as she wandered around the taiga with the Man. She had seen it at night and by day; she had gazed upon it both when it was sunny and when it was covered by snow-laden clouds, and every time she had found it absolutely beautiful. She would look up and feel its deepest breath. There was nothing harmful coming from it – quite the opposite, in fact. That breath gave her peace and quiet.

'Maybe there is another sky – a smaller, darker one,' said the Tiger. 'A sky we're not able to see.'

'Yes, perhaps there is something that eludes even the sky, and whatever eludes the sky eludes us too. It's not the night but a shadow. And in this shadow something is at work that should not be.'

The hut was engulfed in the deep silence of the snow. The Man lay down next to the Tiger and confessed that, in the presence of the despair of a mother who was losing her child, he behaved exactly like his father and grandfather, the shamans.

'I can't help it. They come here after a long journey, helpless, exhausted, bearing their small gifts, and as soon as our eyes meet I see the bright light of hope shining. They expect something from me – how on Earth could I ever disappoint them?'

The fire in the hut was dying, but the Man didn't seem to be cold.

'When I was younger, I was firmer. I chose not to deceive them: I would send them away, telling them that I couldn't help them, that it was not my place to save lives, and invited them to take their gifts back. But the sight of their curved backs walking away would haunt me for days, keeping me awake at night. With my words, with my own arrogant presence, I had extinguished the power of the maternal love that shone so desperately inside them. I had put my ideas in the place of my heart, and this had driven me towards the Sky of the Shadow.'

At that point, the Man sighed and stood up to rekindle the fire in the stove.

'In the end, I think this is exactly what alienates us from the Great Harmony: instead of welcoming and embracing, we keep making our small, pitiful calculations. This is good; that is not. I wonder, at times, who or what we think we are.'

'We tigers think we are tigers,' replied the Tiger, who still had a long way to go before she could fully understand what the Man was saying.

'For us humans it is much more complicated to try to be profoundly human.'

Shivering, the Man wrapped himself in the fur he used as a blanket and resumed his tale.

'The first few times, I was distraught. I would sprinkle water on the child with a leafy branch or with one of the child's belongings if they had brought any, and, while I uttered the mantra, I told myself that I was deceiving them. But then I felt warmth return to the mother's hands; I saw her eyes flooded by the intensity of her gratitude; and I felt that none of that could possibly hurt her.'

The Man's eyes glowed in the dark.

'At times, however, something incredible happened. The child went home healed, holding their mother's hand.'

'That means you truly do have powers.'

'The only power I have is to ask. The pain of the mothers becomes my own, and I offer that pain to the sky, asking for it to be dissolved.'

That night, feeling the Man's back against her own, their breaths synchronized like bellows, the Tiger struggled to fall asleep. Many of the things the Man had said kept echoing inside her. Not having borne any offspring yet, she wondered what her greatest sorrow might possibly be. Certainly not death, since she had long before worked out that when death comes, life ceases to exist. She felt the Man's body beside her and suddenly realized that he had become much feebler over the last year.

I was alone before, but now I'm no longer alone. If he dies, she thought, *then this will be for me the greatest sorrow.*

CHAPTER TWELVE

That Fateful Day

In the years that followed, the Tiger found herself reliving every minute and every hour of that fateful day.

The early summer sun had already dried the mud left from the thaw. The trees were covered with fresh leaves and the tender green of their youth glowed brightly against the blue sky. The air was abuzz with the singing of birds that chased and courted each other in the trees.

After the long winter months, even the Man seemed more cheerful than usual. They had gone out together just before sunrise to collect the flowers of a specific shrub that had healing properties for certain diseases.

Along the way, the Tiger saw butterflies flutter around and felt the impulse to chase them as she had done when she was little.

'Why don't you?' the Man encouraged her, reading her mind.

'I'm too old,' the Tiger replied, embarrassed.

'Innocence is ageless,' the Man said, and then began to sing.

His voice sounded childlike. He continued singing on their way back, as he carried two bags full of flowers.

'Is there something in particular that makes you happy?' the Tiger asked him.

The Man paused for a moment and gestured widely at the sky above.

'That can make you happy?' asked the Tiger.

'Is that not enough for you?'

Was it perhaps his singing that prevented him from hearing? Or old age? Was it that sudden euphoria that made him so distracted? Why did something happen then that should never have happened?

Back at the hut, the Man gently laid the flowers on a plank to let them dry under the large canopy that served as a shelter for the firewood, while the Tiger went inside to rest.

She was just about to lie down when she heard voices.

The voices of human strangers.

She cowered in the darkest corner of the hut and

listened as the Man returned their greeting. From the tone of their voices, they didn't seem to be sick people in need of help.

What had brought them here?

Maybe the Man knew them and was expecting them. But if that were the case, why hadn't he warned her? Why hadn't he sent her to her den as usual?

A strong smell of alcohol wafted up her nostrils. Alarmed, the Tiger sat still, listening.

For a while she heard them talk about the weather, like humans often do when they meet, then one of the visitors said in a low voice:

'We know you have a tiger that does your bidding like a cat. They say its fur is magnificent. We have come to offer you a bargain.'

The Tiger had no idea what a bargain was, but she heard the Man's voice hardening.

'The Tiger is not for sale,' he said curtly, 'and she only does her own bidding.'

'With the money we are offering you,' the larger visitor insisted, 'you could finally buy a house in the village and give up this miserable life.'

'And if you wanted to perform with her, you could get really rich,' suggested a third man, with a purple face.

'I don't need anything,' replied the Man.

The men kept trying to convince him, luring him with new prospects of wealth and income, but the Man put a stop to their flood of words.

'The Tiger is not for sale!'

At that, one of the men stood up abruptly, while another gave a violent kick to the water bucket, yelling: 'You stubborn old man! Stupid, stubborn old man! You're going to regret this!'

Through a crack in the door, the Tiger watched the strangers walk away, swearing and gesticulating, while the Man sat on his old chair just outside the door. She saw him pull the pipe from his jacket and light it calmly, as if nothing had happened.

She, meanwhile, had never felt so confused in her whole existence. Some real humans had come – humans of the kind that filled the Man's heart with pain. They had found them, and things would never go back to the way they were.

She approached the threshold with cautious steps.

'Now what?' she wanted to ask the Man, but before she could utter the words, the glade echoed with the sharp crack of gunfire.

The first thing the Tiger saw was the pipe falling, then the Man's head reclining as a red stain spread across his leather jacket, just above his heart.

A stain that resembled a flower, and that kept expanding on each side.

The Man's eyes were now closed, just like when he slept, but his lips were smiling.

'What an idiot!' she heard the men say. 'Stupid old man, you just died to save a beast.'

'A beast that would have made you rich.'

They were approaching the hut again, with guns ablaze this time, ready to fire.

At that moment, the Tiger remembered she was a tiger. Instead of waiting for them to come to her, she gathered all her strength and sprang from the hut with a fearsome roar.

The first one to shoot was the largest of them; he hit her mid-flight.

His purple face and bloodstained boots were the last things the Tiger saw before darkness descended within her.

CHAPTER THIRTEEN

Welcome to the Circus!

How many noises, how many smells had the Tiger experienced in her life before that moment? Those in her den, when her little cub's eyes were yet to open to the light of the world. Then those in the hissing wind of the taiga, as she wandered around in search of her Kingdom. That wind buffeted her ears relentlessly, cutting through her fur like a thousand ice blades. And then the slow breathing of the earth upon which the hut was built. The storm outside, and the joyful crackling of the stove.

But what she felt now was something she truly couldn't decipher.

She had slept – of that she was certain – but the kind of sleep she was waking up from was different from what she had experienced in the past. She couldn't hear the noise of the forest, nor could she hear the slight rustling sounds the Man made as he slept by her side. She felt cold coming from below her belly, but a very different cold from the snow.

It was a dead, unstable cold.

Her body was bouncing as if she were riding the rapids of a river on a tree trunk.

'Man?' she whispered softly, with her eyes closed. 'Man?'

Nobody answered.

She opened her eyes, but she saw nothing – around her it was pitch black.

What was happening?

She was filled with a great agitation. Could that be death, perhaps?

All of a sudden, the shaking and jerking ceased, and the Tiger heard a hustling and bustling, mixed with muffled human voices.

When the hatch opened, letting the light in, the Tiger roared and leaped up towards the source of the light, but her muzzle bumped into something cold and hard that was holding her captive.

She couldn't understand what it was.

She heard some humans laugh.

Two of them had a rifle in their hands; others approached the truck holding tools and began to assemble something.

When the steel tunnel was ready, the bars that held her prisoner were raised and the Tiger felt the walls of the truck rattle under hard blows. She got up, keeping her head low and her belly flattened, and darted through the space that had opened up in front of her.

Applause greeted her exit.

'Welcome! Welcome to the circus!'

It was a travelling circus, which had three other tigers aside from her. They were older than her, and two of them had never known freedom. The third had lived in a tropical jungle long before.

The next morning, the Tiger was carried in a special cage to where a human was waiting for her, whip in hand.

He was very different from the Man of the hut.

'I know you're a clever tiger. Now show me!' he told her, waving a flaming torch at her.

In response, the Tiger crouched low to the ground, roaring with all the power she could muster.

'What does he want from me?' the Tiger asked her companions later that night.

'The simplest thing. He wants you to obey him.'

'I had a man friend once.'

The old tigers roared with laughter.

'Impossible! Humans either kill you or order you around. There is no other way.'

'Learn to jump through a ring of fire, learn to sit down on cue, and your life will become a walk in the park,' the oldest tiger advised her.

'A walk...?' echoed the Tiger, bewildered.

'Yes,' the others replied in unison. 'Comfortable, easy and safe. Plenty of food and no danger.'

The Tiger remembered the scent of the taiga. That scent was the smell of freedom. She crouched in a corner of the cage and looked sadly at her companions.

That kind of talking wasn't worthy of a tiger.

For a few days, she didn't even feel like roaring. The pain she felt was much more intense than the strongest pain she could have imagined. The Man, the only creature who had managed to break through her loneliness and connect with her, was no more. She knew that. He was dead. And he was dead because of her, for her sake: to allow her to live. That fateful day, the thing she feared most in the world, had happened. Along with her friend, the Tiger had also lost the very essence of her nature. Her freedom.

During training sessions, she kept cowering in a corner. The Tamer cracked his whip and waved his torch, but she remained motionless, not showing the slightest reaction.

After a few days, the Tamer abandoned his tools and kneeled down close to her, speaking gently.

'I know how you feel. I'm not a fool and, although you might find it hard to believe, I do love tigers.'

'I could shred you to pieces in a second,' hissed the Tiger.

'It's a risk I take every second,' the Tamer replied. 'And it is a risk that makes me feel more alive every day. You could kill me, of course, but it would be the last thing you do in your life, because you'd be killed a moment later. Such is the law of the circus. Shredding me to pieces might quench your hatred, but it won't give you back your freedom.'

After that brief, honest exchange, the Tiger was left alone in the cage. She didn't see the Tamer again, and her days felt endless.

Twice a day, her soft-bellied companions rushed through the tunnel that led them to the centre of the ring. Every time they would come back buzzing with excitement.

'Did you see the crowd?' they would ask each other, over and over. 'Did you see how enraptured they were?'

'Soon, you too will understand the importance of a cheering crowd,' the oldest tiger told her one evening, in response to her puzzled look.

And so it was with a certain relief that, after some time, the Tiger resumed her training sessions.

Within a few months, she learned to do everything she was taught.

'You really are a clever tiger,' the Tamer told her one day, as he scratched her behind the ear to show his appreciation.

Her debut was scheduled shortly afterwards, to coincide with the circus's arrival in a Big City. Everywhere, in streets and squares, colourful posters invited people to come to the show. The menacing picture of a roaring tiger, with jaws gaping so wide that you could see all the way down its throat, loomed over a large headline that read:

THE BLOODTHIRSTY SIBERIAN TIGER!
DON'T MISS IT!

That night, the circus was packed. The Tamer wore leather bracers on his wrists, and the lights were dazzling.

'Behold the Terror of the Taiga!' shouted a man with a sparkling jacket.

Nobody laughed at her entrance; no one moved when she roared.

She performed all the tricks without a single glitch and, as soon as she finished the last trick, the tent erupted in applause.

As she returned to her cage, the Tiger found it

hard to calm down, just as she had seen it was for her companions.

'Don't fool yourself,' the oldest tiger told her. 'The applause is not for you, but for the brave Tamer who managed to turn you into a puppet. Today they applaud you; tomorrow, sooner than you think, they'll applaud another tiger.'

How much time had passed? Months? Years?

The wheels of the trailer on which they were transported were replaced several times, and one day the oldest tiger disappeared from the cage.

The Tiger was vaguely aware of the seasons, as she watched the changing landscapes speeding past her during the long journeys in their caravan. Did the trees have leaves, or did they not? At first, she would notice such things, but her attention span kept growing increasingly short. Nothing that was happening in the free world concerned her any more.

Every now and then, some fragments would emerge from her memory of her life with the Man of the hut. Something he had said, one of his expressions, or the way they had chased each other in the snow during a moment of carefree play. She never allowed that door to remain open for too long, though, because it caused her too much sadness.

That world no longer existed, and she would

never be able to return to it. The mere memory would cause her to crouch at the bottom of the cage, with her tail curled around her body.

Seeing her like that, the circus guardians often thought she was sick. Her life was now a succession of repeated actions: waiting for her cage to be cleaned, training, eating, performing in the show and then returning to her cage again.

Whenever the circus remained in a city for a longer stay, the audience would come to see the animals in their cages, just like at the zoo.

The Tiger would see an endless procession of people parading past the bars. Some would flinch, intimidated by her might and her roars. Others, however, enjoyed mocking her, tossing coins at her, or litter or food she couldn't eat, like peanuts.

At first, the Tiger would rage, thrashing against the bars and rattling the trailer with a loud crash of metal.

Later, as she realized these reactions only excited her tormentors more, she recoiled in the furthest corner of the cage, offering only a glimpse of her fur to those who taunted her.

In this parade of humans of all ages, she never made eye contact with anyone, nor did she hear a voice that was similar to the Man's.

Except on one occasion.

'Tiger...?' she heard a little girl whisper softly, with a voice that came from her heart.

'Yes?' she replied, lifting her head in the hope of meeting the eyes of whoever had spoken, but the little girl had already been dragged away.

'The tigers are boring – they don't do anything. Come on, let's go to see the apes.'

CHAPTER FOURTEEN

The Little Acrobat

How many times had the words of the Man echoed in the Tiger's mind while the screaming audience walked past her?

'Having eyes and looking are not the same thing.'

'What do you mean?'

'Eyes are related to the hands, while looking is related to the heart. Looking knows no distances or obstacles. The eyes, meanwhile, measure everything. If they find an empty space, they build a wall right there and then.'

'How can I tell them apart?'

'The heart talks straight to the heart, without any need for lips' had been the Man's answer.

How many hearts had she met during those years?

None, apart from the fleeting glimpse of that little girl's.

The Tiger felt worn out by the eyes that had lingered on her fur. On the days when there was no show, a deep weariness invaded every fibre of her being.

What had become of all her ambitions?

She had left her home and headed Eastwards, searching for a greater destiny, but her fate was now confined to the boundaries of the cage. At first, she had paced back and forth, day and night, never stopping, walking for hours without going anywhere. Four steps forward, turn around, four steps back.

'We've all done that!' the other tigers had told her. 'You'll calm down too, you'll see. Oh yes, you will.'

They were right.

She had indeed calmed down, and now she spent all her time crouching in a corner of the cage. But it was a calm very different from that of an ocean, which, in its most secret depths, harbours the frightening power of a wave capable of destroying everything.

Where had she gone wrong?

Was it she who had made a mistake, or had Fate turned its back on her?

The Man's sacrifice had been for nothing.

Either way, everything had gone wrong. She had been captured and he was dead. If only he'd accepted the money. Then he would still be alive and she wouldn't be alone in this world once again.

But could she ever return to someone who had traded her life for a handful of coins? Wouldn't she have felt even more desperately lonely if, in addition to captivity, she'd had to endure the terrible loneliness of betrayal?

Is there a more potent poison?

You give yourself to someone in complete innocence, and they seem to reciprocate, but they have other plans. There's a secret motive in their actions and you never realize it until it's too late.

The Tiger was engrossed in these thoughts when a voice echoed in her heart.

'Are you a sad tiger?'

She stood up, looking around.

There didn't seem to be anyone in sight.

It was only when she leaned over the bars of her trailer that she saw a child, staring up at her from down below.

'Are you the one talking?' she asked.

'Yes,' the child replied.

'I've never seen you before.'

'I arrived yesterday.'

The Tiger felt a rush of words erupting from her heart.

'Where do you come from? Are you alone?'

'I'm here with my family,' said the boy. 'We're acrobats and we come from a town beyond the taiga.'

The taiga!

Just hearing that word, the Tiger felt her heart pound. How long had it been since her paws had rested in the snow, on ice, on the moss drenched with water? Cement and sawdust, sawdust and cement; for too many years this had ruled her life. How long had it been since she had really seen the stars and breathed snow from her nostrils? How long had it been since she had felt her whiskers freeze?

'I come from there too!' she cried with a new energy.

'I know,' the boy replied. 'It's written here below – that's why I told you.'

Then, with a light step, he headed towards the circus tent and disappeared inside.

That night, the Tiger dreamed of the Man for the first time in a long while. He wasn't saying or doing anything in particular. He was just sitting next to the stove, as he often had during the winter. The light that emanated from his body lingered in the eyes of the Tiger for a long time. She was now awake and she could still see it – or, better yet, feel it deep within her heart.

Where did that light come from?

It looked like the light of dawn, but it was brighter than the brightest sunrise.

As she awoke the next morning, the Tiger realized she wasn't sad any more. She stood up and stretched, shaking her body several times as if it were covered with snow.

She was no longer alone.

There was a child, and that child had looked at her.

Not only that, but he even came from a world not far from her own. If she said 'snow', he would understand – as he would if she added, 'I can run for days without encountering anything.'

A week later, she discovered that the acrobats and tigers practised at the same time. They were down below and the athletes were up above, suspended in the air. There was only an elastic net between them.

So often she would get distracted during her routines' jumps and roars. The child's parents would dangle from the trapezes and then, suddenly, they'd let go and their bodies would slice through the air as if the ground weren't dragging them down, as if they were weightless. There was always someone on the other side who would grab them by the wrists or ankles. Even the child, one day, would jump like that – light as a feather, blissfully confident in the grip of his parents.

It takes trust to jump into the void, the Tiger thought, leaping into the flaming circle. *I simply hop from stool to stool, just like I once leaped upon the backs of the deer. In all these years I have learned nothing. I allowed the bars to enter my heart, blocking any way out.*

'We are the first jailers of ourselves.'

Weren't these the words of the Man?

Her fate had changed abruptly, but she had almost immediately surrendered to her new situation.

The routine, the anger, the cage.

The circus had been her only horizon up until that moment. Her days divided equally between boredom and resentment; her soul transformed into a scarecrow made of tiger fur. A fur that was worn out now, listless, frayed.

This was not how she'd imagined her life when she began her journey to the East. The captivity in the circus had turned her dreams into wet sawdust.

Since the arrival of the acrobats, however, something had changed. She no longer slept so dreadfully at night, and a light had begun to creep into her daytime rest too. Not the cold light of the neon, but the warm light of the oil lamp inside the hut.

Once, the Man had created some wonderful images simply by playing with the shadows of his hands on the wall.

The Tiger was left breathless just looking at them. She had never thought it were possible to see something that did not visibly exist.

'The gift of vision,' the Man had told her, 'is the greatest of gifts.'

CHAPTER FIFTEEN

I Want to Learn to Fly

The journeys weren't journeys any more; the shows weren't shows. The long hours spent travelling in the caravan along the roads increased, and somehow she was no longer affected by the anticipation she usually felt before entering the circus ring, or by the voice of the Presenter shouting, 'The fearsome Siberian tiger!' as all her muscles sprang into action to run the short distance between the tunnel and the stool.

The Tiger was there, but at the same time she wasn't.

She had experienced that before: her mind would function, while her heart remained elsewhere. But, until then, that elsewhere was a world she had lost. The den, her mother, her brother, the taiga, the Man, the hut. It was an elsewhere that made her sad. Ahead of the Tiger lay the opaqueness of a wall, and behind her was a world that faded a little more from her memory each day.

But now, suddenly, the connection had been reversed. The wall had dissolved, just like fog disperses as the sun grows stronger, and through the few remaining droplets she was able to glimpse a brand-new world that was hers to conquer.

The child's voice had shattered her inner prison, allowing her to imagine a reality that was ahead of her rather than behind.

It had taken so little – a question, a glance – for everything to turn upside down.

The Tiger was caught by surprise.

You had to be conflicted, perhaps, in order to change things.

Now she could see the shadows on the wall, and she was certain that, sooner or later, those shadows would have the power to turn into something more tangible.

'Vision brings hope,' the Man had said once, as they walked in the taiga.

The Tiger couldn't understand back then, but now she suddenly knew what he meant. What else is hope, if not a pack of hounds constantly chasing you? They close in on your heels, they hunt you down, forcing you to do one thing only: to run to meet what lies before you.

She had often longed for this.

Clawing, shoving, shredding someone – and reconquering her freedom in this way? For many years this had been her first instinct – and the clearest, the strongest. But it was an instinct that would have led her to a dead end – she knew that.

In fact, there were many stories about escape attempts, passed on among the members of the circus. An elephant, a giraffe, a hippo who couldn't resist the lure of freedom. Their bids for freedom didn't have a particularly glorious conclusion. What sort of freedom could an elephant find among the desolate city outskirts? The freedom to stretch its legs, at most. Taking such a big risk for such a miserable outcome definitely was not worth it.

That's why the Tiger had done nothing – until then.

But everything was different now.

Now she knew where to go, and why.

She wanted to be an acrobat; she wanted to possess grace and lightness. She was tired of leaping from stool to stool as if these stools were the back of some prey. She wanted to learn something different; she wanted to dominate the air instead of the ground. When you have a dream, you can overturn even the tallest mountain. No obstacle feels like an obstacle; no limit a true limit.

During the training sessions, she saw the Little Acrobat jump on a platform and leap upwards, tracing breathtaking trajectories with his body.

'Do you have wings hidden somewhere?' the Tiger asked him one day.

'No, why?'

'When you fly you seem weightless, like a feather.'

'If I were as light as a feather, the air would lead me wherever it wants. It is because I do have a weight that I can land where I want.'

'But how can you fly?'

The Little Acrobat burst out laughing.

'I don't fly – I only move from one spot to the other. You jump from one stool to the next; I jump from one trapeze to another.'

The Tiger remained silent, puzzled. What she had seen happen above her head seemed infinitely more harmonious than what she did every day: brush against the sawdust with her belly. There was a lightness in the Little Acrobat that she had never had. One moment he was standing on the ring, and the next he was vaulting above everyone's head as if it were the most effortless thing in the world.

'What happens if you make a mistake?' the Tiger asked him once.

The Little Acrobat shrugged.

'I fall.'

'And you're not afraid?'

'That's something you learn too. If you want to go high, you have to learn how to fall down first.

We've been acrobats for generations. My parents would throw me in the air when I was just a baby.'

'So, you *can* learn?'

'Of course! You just have to be patient and never give up if a jump goes wrong.'

She would have liked to also ask him whether he was happy doing what he did, but she knew she didn't need to. His eyes gleamed with the sheer joy that he experienced through flying.

'If you have a dream, you have to learn to keep at it,' said the Little Acrobat before leaving. 'Otherwise it remains just a dream.'

The Tiger didn't get a chance to talk to him again for the next few weeks, only encountering him around the circus tent.

Then, on a sweltering summer night that was keeping everyone awake, the Little Acrobat reappeared in front of the trailer.

The Tiger mustered her courage and told him:

'I have a dream too. But I don't know if I can tell you.'

'To eat me?'

'No.'

'Tell me, then.'

'My dream is to become an acrobat.'

'But you jump already. You leap through fire hoops and the flames never even singe your tail.'

'Yes, but only from one side to the other – the

ground is always at the same distance from my belly. I want to learn to do what you do instead. Lifting all my paws from the ground and rising up, as though I were weightless.'

The Little Acrobat remained silent and very still, staring at the Tiger. He had just realized how mangy the Tiger was; how much sadness welled in those eyes that hadn't seen the taiga for so long. He remembered hearing about winged horses, but never about a tiger who could fly.

'So?' urged the Tiger impatiently.

The Little Acrobat saw a new light sparkle in his friend's eyes.

'So, I think you should go somewhere high and try a few jumps. Small jumps at first, and then bigger and bigger.'

'Yes,' she agreed. 'But how do I do that? The roof of the cage is so low.'

The Little Acrobat pondered in silence. 'You're right: you can't fly if there's no room above you.'

'Can you help me?' asked the Tiger in a small voice.

The Little Acrobat thought some more, then smiled and said, 'I can let you out if you want.'

'But there's a chain.'

'Every chain has its key,' he answered.

It all happened incredibly fast, like in a dream.

Two nights later, while everyone was asleep, the

Little Acrobat came back with a large set of keys, finding the right one after a few attempts. Then he removed the thick chain with his tiny hands and just said, 'There!' as he stood by her side.

For a moment, the Tiger was astounded.

The freedom she had craved for so many years was now in front of her, within a paw's reach.

All around her it was dark and still.

She poked her head tentatively out of the cage. Then, looking up, she saw a shooting star streak across the summer sky.

Although the air she breathed was the same as in her cage, it immediately felt different.

For a moment, she pictured everything that could happen as soon as her paws touched the ground: the alarm, guns ablaze everywhere and the despair of the Tamer to whom she had become attached over the years.

But then she remembered her father's stern eyes as he told her, 'You are a tiger!' before disappearing into the forest.

So she jumped down from the trailer.

As soon as she reached the ground, she realized that the Little Acrobat was no taller than she.

They looked into each other's eyes for a long time, in silence.

Then the Tiger came closer, brushing her big head against the child's.

'Your whiskers are tickling me,' the Little Acrobat laughed.

'Goodbye! I will always love you,' the Tiger told him, before she turned around and started running, never looking back.

CHAPTER SIXTEEN

In the City of Humans

What did the Tiger know about the world of humans?

How could she know the extent of the concrete mountains inside which they lived; of the asphalt rivers along which they travelled, like herds? Until then she had been convinced that there was only one road – the one along which the circus caravan travelled – and that all humans lived in those buildings they passed by along the way. She was certain that there was an open horizon somewhere beyond that barrier, and that once she crossed that horizon, she would find herself in her taiga again.

But it wasn't like that.

The buildings were followed by more buildings, and the roads crawling with traffic cut through every space like a tangle of knots, blocking her way.

The first human who saw her jump from one side of the road to the other in the middle of the night probably thought they were hallucinating.

It was only at the crack of dawn, when the circus caretaker noticed the empty cage, that the alarm went off and the news of a savage beast prowling around the city outskirts turned into a reality.

For the first time in her life, the Tiger found out what it meant to be prey. Everyone was hunting her down; everyone wanted to kill her.

The sky was crossed by helicopters and there was no street or back road that wasn't patrolled by groups of armed humans.

Children were forbidden to leave their homes, which drastically reduced her chances of asking for help or even just information. The mere sight of her tail would have drawn gunfire upon her.

There were several incidents in those days. Just wearing something orange and black was enough to draw some lunatic's attention.

The Tiger found herself cursing her fur – so useful in the taiga yet so useless in the outskirts of a city. It would have been much better if her fur were the colour of a rat's.

Luckily, a few miles from the circus, she came across an almost-dry ditch covered by reeds, and there she crouched and waited for nightfall.

As soon as it was dark, she stepped out cautiously, without any idea of where she was going.

The faintest noise would make her hold her breath.

She spent the first three days like that.

Every now and then, her heart filled with gloom.

Had she escaped from her prison only to spend the rest of her days in a ditch, like a frog?

What if that escape was the greatest mistake of her life?

By now, she had started feeling very hungry. Aside from some rats and a snake, she couldn't find anything to eat.

Her body had grown accustomed to regular mealtimes in the circus, and when each one came around her stomach would growl, demanding her daily ration.

She had left behind something she knew, something familiar, to embrace a world unknown. But hadn't she done that when she was young, too? Instead of marking out a territory where she could rule with her offspring, she had ventured East, to find out what lay beyond the horizon. The sun continued rising and setting, seemingly oblivious to everything the Tiger had to endure on her journey to meet it.

After a few more days and nights crawling in the ditch, the Tiger began to suspect she had only walked in circles. The landscape she could see beyond the reeds was always the same.

Not even the smells indicated anything different.

The smell of humans – too many humans.

The smell of engines – too many engines.

The smell of guns too, which occasionally crackled and flashed somewhere around her.

Hearing those shots, the Tiger couldn't help but think of the Man. She had heard that very same noise once before, and she had been alone in the world ever since.

One night, with her belly lying in the mud and a dark, gloomy sky above her, the Tiger thought the only sensible thing to do was to venture outside and meet the humans with their guns.

'Here I am!' she would say, after satisfying herself by devouring a few of them first.

Then they would shoot her with every weapon they had available, and she would die. And they would put their feet on her head, laughing. And everything would finally be over. The running, the escape, the chasing, the hunger, the thirst – and, with it, the feeling that she had always done the wrong thing in her life.

Her body would remain there, on the ground. But what about all that was not her body?

When they were little cubs, their mother, speaking of the tigers that had lived before her, had told them: 'They now walk in the taiga where no blood is shed.'

'Why?' Little Tiger had asked her.

'Because there's no more hunger there.'

'But then,' her brother asked, 'if they don't hunt, what do they do all day?'

Their mother had smiled gently.

'I don't know, but I will some day. And you will too, some day further ahead. All tigers find out eventually, when they leave their fur.'

During the long winters in the hut, the Tiger had asked the Man the same question.

'What happens when you close your eyes and you can't open them any more?'

The Man had remained silent, handling a piece of wood he was carving.

For a while, he went on carving as if he hadn't heard the question.

The Tiger had pressed him. 'Do you know the taiga where no blood is shed?'

The Man had nodded, barely moving his head.

'Is that where we're going?'

Instead of answering, the Man remained absorbed in his thoughts.

Woodchips were falling around him like snow, and a log crackled noisily in the stove.

A strong wind had picked up outside just as they were about to go to sleep.

Only when they were lying next to each other under the large rug did the Man say:

'It depends on the fire you kindle.'

CHAPTER SEVENTEEN

The Rag-Man

When the feeble city sun touched the ditch, the Tiger brushed off the musings of the night. The absence of light brings sad thoughts; when the sun returns, one needs to be brave enough to cast them away.

Besides, what kind of tiger is a tiger that gives up?

Should she be cornered, she would fight tooth and nail. A tiger never lets herself be struck from behind. At the very last moment she turns and lunges, so that she's hit right in the head or the heart. Being shot in the back or the thighs is for deer or wild boars.

But how could she disappoint the Little Acrobat? He had set her free to allow her to pursue her dream, not for her to jump into the arms of her assassins.

With these thoughts in her head and caution in her muffled steps, the Tiger started moving along the ditch.

She bumped into a river rat and devoured it. It tasted like mud, but nonetheless she felt some strength rush through her body.

She moved forward and then stopped, moved some more and stopped again, her ears pricked and ready to pick up any noise, her tail brushing the water's surface.

Suddenly, she heard the voice of a human nearby.

Taken by surprise, she recoiled, snarling.

At first, all she saw was a heap of cartons moving haphazardly, but after a few moments the head of a human covered in rags poked out.

They stared at each other for a moment that felt endless.

With imperceptible movements, the Tiger flinched, her body ready to pounce.

'Are you real?' the Rag-Man asked, rubbing his eyes.

The Tiger noticed he wasn't carrying a weapon.

'I am a tiger,' she answered.

He kept staring at her, taking a few uncertain steps in her direction.

'I see that. It's just that I'm not sure you really exist.'

The Tiger was surprised. That human could understand her, just like the children did.

'What else would I be, then?'

'A vision.'

'A vision?'

'Something that's only inside my head.'

'And why would I be inside your head and not in the ditch?'

The Rag-Man shook his head. 'Because my whole life I've dreamed of meeting a real tiger. Look,' he said, rolling up the sleeve of his shirt, 'I even have one tattooed on my arm.'

The Tiger leaned forward slightly and saw the faded image of one of her kin painted on the man's skin.

'I wanted to be a tiger,' he continued, lowering his gaze. 'I dreamed about it as a child. I wanted to be the strongest, the bravest, the most noble.'

'Why would you want that? It's not easy being a tiger.'

'It's not easy being human, either.'

The two fell silent for a while.

The Tiger pondered the Rag-Man's words. She knew what it meant to be strong and also to be brave, but she didn't understand what it meant to be noble.

'Noble?' she repeated softly.

'Yes. Only you tigers can act without self-interest. You are a Queen. You don't need to make anyone like you. You go your own way; you eat what you need to eat. There's no room in your life for fake business – everything you do is genuine.'

'That's why you wanted to be a tiger?'

'Yes, because that's how I felt inside. I've never had a hidden agenda in my heart.'

'And that is noble?'

The Rag-Man nodded, then took his head between his hands, sighing. 'I hadn't realized that most humans have the heart of a baboon rather than a tiger. They are all flattery and smiles, masking a poison that flows freely. And why is that? For power. Power for a day, a month, a year. How can anything built on pettiness truly last? There is always someone pettier than you ready to step forward. I've been a fool. Instead of a tiger, I've become a loser.'

'A loser?'

The Tiger couldn't understand.

The Rag-Man wiped his eyes with the back of his hand. 'Yes, a loser. Someone who lives in a ditch dressed in rags, with a cardboard roof over his head.'

The Tiger knew that feeling all too well. Instead of choosing the right path, she felt that she had always taken the wrong one. Some fates were truly alike, she thought. They weren't born in the same den – she and the Rag-Man – but it felt as if they were siblings.

'Are you hiding a weapon?' the Tiger asked, as a precaution.

The Rag-Man pulled a tiny pocketknife out of his jacket. 'Just this.'

'Come closer then.'

'Do you want to eat me?'

'No, I want to prove to you that I am real.'

Hesitating, the Rag-Man moved closer.

'Reach out and touch me!' the Tiger encouraged him.

The Rag-Man complied, his hand shaking like a birch tree rocked by the wind.

'It's beautiful…' he whispered, sinking his fingers into the Tiger's thick fur. 'Beautiful.' Then, in a childlike voice, he asked, 'May I hug you?'

'You may,' replied the Tiger.

The Rag-Man wrapped his arms around that mighty neck, burying his face in the striped fur. He remained like that for a long time, his body shaken by little gasps. The Tiger felt water dropping on her fur. It felt like rain, but it was slightly warm instead of cold. It was running down from the Rag-Man's eyes.

It was the first time she ever saw tears.

'I didn't make it,' the Rag-Man kept repeating in a sad chant. 'I didn't make it. I wanted to be a tiger, but I let myself be overpowered by baboons instead.'

The Tiger waited patiently for the tears to stop, then said, 'If you help a tiger, you will become a tiger yourself.'

The Rag-Man lifted his face from the Tiger's fur. His eyes were red and swollen, but in the depths something was beginning to sparkle that didn't look like despair at all. It was no longer the look of a man

behind bars: it was that of a free man, one beyond bars.

'Everyone wants to kill me,' whispered the Tiger after a while.

'But I won't let them,' the Rag-Man exclaimed with a voice that sounded like a roar, springing up with unexpected energy.

Later, they sat down together to concoct a plan. Those bloodthirsty humans who wanted to capture her were no different from a pack of hounds, after all: they ran wherever they caught scent of a track, or wherever one might be.

The important thing was to let them believe that *was* the case.

The Rag-Man used his pocketknife to cut off a tuft of the Tiger's fur. She, in turn, ripped the flaps of his jackets and his shirt with her teeth, then drew long, red marks on the face and neck of her new friend with her claws.

Their eyes met.

The Rag-Man was crying again. 'Now I know that my whole life I was just waiting for you.'

'Whoever saves a tiger is also a tiger.'

Before setting off to accomplish his mission, the Rag-Man hugged the Tiger tightly, telling her not to move until sunset. That would give him time to reach the opposite side of city, where he would set their plan in motion.

When the first evening shadows fell, he would jump from behind a bush, looking distraught and screaming: 'Help! The tiger attacked me! It's a miracle I'm alive!'

The tuft of hair and the scratches on his face would confirm that he wasn't drunk.

'Which way did it go?' they would ask him.

Then he would shout: 'Towards the sea! Towards the sea!'

And so it happened.

The following night, while the Tiger ran at breakneck speed towards the mountains, with the rediscovered energy of her youth, the road leading to the sea filled with cars and helicopters crowded the sky, risking collision as they flew.

CHAPTER EIGHTEEN

Towards Freedom

How long had she been running?

She couldn't tell.

The sun had risen and set several times. At night, the Tiger sought refuge in the bush; by day, she ran towards the mountains that stood high on the horizon. As she ran, her body gradually shed the heaviness of captivity. Merely jumping from stool to stool had caused her muscles to waste away and her lungs to become weak.

The Tiger knew she was no longer young, but as she ran, faster and faster, she felt as if she were regaining a part of her life.

The Earth was emanating its scent, and so was the sky.

The scent of rain, of lightning.

The scent of the sun that warms up all things on Earth.

Each evening, when she looked back from her hiding place at the road she had travelled that day, she saw that the city of the humans had grown smaller. Its bright lights twinkled in the night, projecting a faint arc that was suspended in the sky – until one evening, when, turning around, she saw that even that faint glow had disappeared.

Behind her lay the plains; ahead, the mountains.

During her life as a free tiger, she had spent many years running towards the horizon, never quite managing to reach it. Now she seemed to have arrived. By running and running, she had finally reached the furthest point. But, yet again, even that point seemed to hold nothing for her.

Ahead of her she saw trees, trees and more trees. Trees that grew uphill rather than on flat land. And then rocks, and more rocks, that stood tall like an impassable barrier.

The rocks almost reached the sky, but they were not the sky. It was impossible for the Tiger to know what lay beyond those rocks, just as it was impossible to know where the sun went when it disappeared behind the trees in the taiga, and why it always rose from the opposite side.

Once again, the Tiger felt compelled to keep moving forward.

The first forests she crossed weren't very different from those she had known in her youth. Firs, firs and more firs, and the smell of resin that permeates the air on hot days.

In the clearings, she saw boundless prey grazing quietly beyond a wall. It would have been very easy for her to eat one. Easy, but dangerous, because the humans would notice the signs of her passage and a big hunt would be moved to the mountains.

It was better to settle for the smaller creatures: hares, foxes, anything that would allow her to move forward without leaving a trace.

When the trees started thinning out on the mountain ridges, the Tiger stopped. There were no signs of human presence, aside from the thin plume of smoke rising from a woodcutter's hut lower down.

The feeling of fatigue after the long journey and the emotions of the last few days were beginning to take their toll. The Tiger had a new obstacle to overcome, right in front of her. Its peaks stood high against the sky.

She was unsure what to do.

Turning back was pointless, but was there really any point in trying to go on? Tigers are not built to climb rocky mountains. Their paws are too big, their bodies too heavy. Their pads are perfectly suited to walk on snowy surfaces, on moss, lichens and leaves, but not on bare rocks. Even her long tail would be of little use, as unlike a squirrel's tail it wasn't designed to help her keep her balance. Attempting to climb the mountain might end up being no more than the last in her long list of failures.

As a terrifying ravine opened up suddenly before her, she would find herself repeating: 'I didn't make it! I didn't make it!' like the Rag-Man.

But nobody would hear her; her paws would start losing their grip, and as she tried desperately to cling to thin air, she would fall into the ravine.

What would be left of her then?

A few scratch marks on the mountainside. Food for crows, splattered at the bottom. Maybe a poster or two with her picture on, forgotten at the bottom of some box at the circus...the bloodthirsty Siberian tiger.

But, ultimately, wasn't that how all creatures ended up – as food for someone else? Was there anything else beyond that?

As she rested on a carpet of pine needles, the Tiger thought about how she had managed to disappoint even the Tamer. They had worked together for years.

'You're my pride,' he would often whisper in her ear at the end of a show.

It was true that the Tamer loved tigers; he understood them. But what do you call the kind of love that sacrifices the freedom of another?

At that moment, she realized she was feeling nostalgic for her life at the circus. Not for the bars and cages, of course, but for the roaring applause that greeted her appearance on the stage, for the audience holding their breath in anticipation as she prepared to leap through the flaming hoops.

Was dreaming of the freedom of flying just another crazy idea? She was old and heavy, and the only thing she had to look forward to was an impassable mountain range. The lightness of the Little Acrobat would never be hers.

And yet, if she were to be born again, what would her fate be?

In a few years, the Tamer's belly would have grown even larger. He hadn't been the handsome young fellow coveted by all the ladies for quite some time now.

And the same had happened to her. The boredom of captivity and the comfort she found in food had weighed her down, and the magnificent black and orange stripes of her coat had begun to lose their lustre. Soon the skin of her belly would sag down to the ground and her roars would no longer scare anyone. People would see her rotting teeth, her tongue coated with a white glaze from eating too many chickens. Instead of applauding, they would shout: 'Look at that mangy tiger!'

Her master would then start to diet, and he

would put her on a diet too. Instead of fresh beef steaks, she would be given only pellets.

Then, one day, when her paws were no longer strong enough for her to leap through the hoops – the day when even climbing on her stool would take too much effort – the Doctor would appear at the door of her cage.

He was a nice man, the Doctor. He had been caring for her for many years, and he smelled good too. He would walk inside and say, 'How's it going, old girl?', gently scratching her between the ears.

The Tamer would appear behind the Doctor, his hair now completely white and his large belly bulging out of his ratty suit. His booming voice wouldn't have its normal cheerful tone, but would be slightly shaky, cracking with sadness.

Intrigued, the Tiger would look at him with renewed interest and notice something she'd rather not see. The Tamer's eyes – those eyes she knew so well – would be clouded over and watery. They would well up with a flood of tears that he could hardly hold back. Then, and only then, would she finally realize. As they would say, her time had come.

Igor, the bear that had danced the cha-cha-cha for so many years, wiggling his huge body for the audience's amusement, had met a similar fate. The Doctor had given him a shot as he lay on the ground, and his huge paws had flailed around for a few seconds – his last dance – and then he had remained motionless, like a giant boulder, his fur matted, the flies already feasting on his nose and eyes without him even bothering to wave them away.

A bulldozer had arrived a few minutes later. With a great deal of effort and a lot of fuss, some workers had picked up Igor's body, and he had disappeared from the circus for ever.

The same thing would happen to her. The Doctor would fiddle about with his tubes, while the Tamer stroked her paw, whispering through his tears, 'Goodbye, old girl. You've been the best.'

With a final twitch, she would open her mouth to try to resist – to escape, to maul everyone. But instead of a roar, she would manage only a miaow. In that very moment, the large syringe would pierce the sagging skin of her neck, bringing eternal darkness to her mind and heart.

Is this really what I want? the Tiger wondered, lying down at the edge of the forest.

How could she regret such a miserable fate? It would be a thousand times better to become food for the crows and the foxes.

While the Tiger was engrossed in these thoughts, the sunlight started to flood the tallest mountain peaks. The valley down below was still immersed in darkness, while up there a rosy light embraced even the tiniest rock fragment.

How different it was from the sun that rose above the taiga! As much as that sun had looked like you could reach out and touch it with your paw, this one was clearly well beyond her reach.

As the light finally filled every corner, the Tiger realized she was thirsty. She didn't have to walk far to find a river. It flowed wildly among the rocks in twists and jumps and turns, with the occasional small bend where the flow was gentler.

The Tiger leaned over one such bend and saw her image reflected on the water's surface. She could see the dark silhouettes of fish trying to resist the current below her wide-eyed reflection. It had been so long since she had seen herself! The bowls in her circus trailer had reflected only their metallic base.

Just as there is a horizon in the sky, thought the Tiger, *there must be a horizon in the water. It is the life in water that reflects the living.*

She drank some more and then stood motionless, looking at herself.

How long had it been since she had first discovered her own reflection?

Their mother had taken them down to the river that first time. The Tiger still remembered her words: 'Don't be afraid! What you see is your face. Always be worthy of what you see.'

Hearing her mother's voice inside her head, she suddenly felt weak. She crouched down, touching the water with her front paws.

How much time had passed since she had begun her journey to find her?

Where was her mother now?

Would the Tiger be able to see her, just as she was able to hear her voice?

'Between those who give life and those who receive it there is a thread that never breaks,' her mother had told her once.

At the time, the Tiger couldn't understand whether that was a good or a bad thing.

Was she worthy of the image she had seen reflected in the water many years before, she wondered, or had she betrayed it?

And what kind of image was it, after all?

The image of someone who was very thirsty.

She had come there only to drink, just as she had done when she was young – just as she was doing now, as she leaned over the river.

I am thirsty, thought the Tiger after a while. *I've been looking for water my whole life, but none of the water I have found has managed to quench my thirst.*

'Yours is not the kind of thirst that water can quench,' the Man of the hut had once told her.

'Wonder creates space for questions inside you, and questions are like the raging waters of a river. You cannot stop them; you can never catch a drop and say, "This really is the last one." '

The sun was now at its peak, and there were no clouds in the sky. The birds chirped, calling to each other from between the branches of the last fir trees, while bees buzzed over the flowers in the grass.

The Tiger took one more sip of water, and then, lurking in the shadows, she splashed the water loudly as she tried to catch some fish.

When she was finally sated, she moved away from the river, walking towards the mountains.

What lay beyond them?

Wasn't that what she had wanted to know from the very beginning? Things as they seem; things as they are.

CHAPTER NINETEEN

The Wall to Climb

Instead of starting to climb straight away, the Tiger searched for a smoother path to the peak, first through the higher pastures and then along the foothills where a few solitary trees still stood, mighty and majestic.

Driven by hunger, she ventured out on to the scree slopes every now and then to hunt down large, horned prey, or fat little creatures that disappeared under the rocks, hearing the sound of many – too many – stones and pebbles scatter beneath her paws like the balls that the monkeys tossed in their circus tricks.

The Tiger wasn't accustomed to feeling the ground slide around underneath her paws; she growled as she walked, as if there were some hidden enemy nearby. She climbed up and then slid back down. She tried climbing again, and down she went once more.

One of the things a tiger can always count on is their steady step. If their step falters, the whole world starts to sway.

How much more will I have to endure? she wondered. *I wanted to discover the mystery of the sun, and I ended up in a cage.*

I wanted to become an acrobat, and instead I ended up being a clown. If I were still in the circus, they would all laugh at me. Is there anything more laughable than ferocity that stumbles, unable to stand steady on her own legs?

It was while trying to catch a marmot one day that she tumbled downhill, dragging hundreds of stones along with her. Some of the stones struck her on the head as she fell, leaving her unconscious at the bottom of the scree.

When she came back to her senses and opened her eyes to see the huge rock towering above her, the words of the Man of the hut came to her mind.

'Sad are those lives that never meet a wall to climb.'

Back then, the Tiger didn't have the faintest idea what a wall could be. The taiga was flat and seemingly endless. There were no obstacles on the horizon.

'What is a wall?' she had asked.

'It's an obstacle that stands in your way.'

That day they were out foraging for berries, and she didn't feel like asking any more questions. In the evening, however, lying on the rug, she couldn't help asking the Man the reason why anyone should be sad about not finding obstacles on their path.

'A mushroom lives a mushroom's life; a bee lives the life of a bee; and a tree a tree,' he replied. 'The same goes for stones, water and clouds. Even lightning lives its own life, and so does hail. But everything changes when it comes to humans.'

'Why?' she asked softly.

The wind was very strong that night. It pierced through the logs in the walls of the hut, shaking it fiercely as if trying to blow it away. The windows rattled, and everything that was not fixed down trembled and swayed: the lantern, the bucket, the rifle, the pitcher balanced precariously on the stove.

For a while, the rattling and swaying were the only answers to her question. She was convinced the Man was already asleep when she heard his voice in the dark:

'A treasure is never found lying on your doorstep.'

That night, the Tiger had struggled to fall asleep. She was still young then, and inexperienced. For two whole seasons she had done nothing but walk far and wide across the taiga.

As she looked back on those days, she tried to remember whether she had ever met a real obstacle. Rivers, of course. Treacherous waterways covered in ice or flowing wildly with the powerful tides of the thaw. Rivers, however, only needed to be crossed. You had to be skilful – there were indeed many dangers – but once you'd crossed, the landscape was identical to that which you had left on the other side.

A river was no wall, then.

Early one morning, as she slept lightly, she saw her mother's eyes again. She wore the same attentive expression as she had while keeping watch over her sleeping cubs. It was because of her mother that the Tiger had started her journey. The Tiger didn't have to climb a wall to go to look for her, but she had still left behind everything she knew in order to face the unknown.

There was a gaping void in her heart, right where her mother used to be. No Kingdom could ever have filled it.

Nothing she knew had the power to fill that absence.

The next evening, while the storm still raged, she had asked the Man to tell her more about the wall.

'There are walls you climb with your hands, and others you climb with your heart,' he had replied. 'Just as there are creatures that know only the monotony of the flatlands, and others that are always compelled to climb.'

Then the Man sat down on the rug and put a piece of wood in the stove, telling her as he did so about the steep wall he had had to climb in the course of his life.

A long time ago, when he was young, he had had a wife; a dearly beloved wife. That wife was pregnant with his child, but just before the child was born, they had both been killed by a drunk robber. In just a few seconds, everything he held most dear, everything that gave purpose and hope to his life, had been wiped away. Blood fell on the snow, and the body of his beloved wife turned into a lifeless puppet.

Where would he ever find her gaze or her breath again?

How could he know what his child's eyes looked like – those eyes that would never open to see the world?

'I had two choices before me. Go on a killing spree and murder all the robbers I found, or face the wall, retire and try to understand. Neither would give me back what I had lost, but while one choice would only cause more pain and bloodshed, the other could perhaps lead me to understand the meaning of what had happened to me. I wasn't by any means certain – it was only a hope.'

'Hope?' The Tiger had never heard that word. 'What is that?'

'It is the humble power that carries the world forward.'

Back then, the Tiger couldn't understand the meaning of those words, but now that most of her life was behind her, she recognized the truth in what the Man had said.

Wasn't it the hope of finding her mother that had led her to leave the certainty of the Kingdom? And why had she abandoned the reassuring routine of the circus if not for the hope of regaining the dignity of her early days?

Only stones can survive without an inner life. Everything else – everything that lives – is driven and defined by hope.

CHAPTER TWENTY

The Walnut and the Shell

For over a year, the Tiger lived between high-altitude grasslands and scree slopes at the foot of the great rocky walls of the snow-capped mountains. She had arrived together with the spring blooms; she had faced the mild summer warmth and the short, violent thunderstorm that drenched every single hair in her fur. Then the days had begun to shorten, the grass had become yellow and the snow had made its appearance over the highest peaks and valleys.

She had missed the snow so much!

Narrowing her eyes, she was able to catch its scent even from miles away. She recognized its texture as easily as if it were beneath her paws.

Frozen. Less frozen. Soft. Almost melted.

Seeing the snow again brought an unexpected feeling of peace to her heart.

Instead of walking tirelessly back and forth – a habit from her long years in the circus that had somehow stuck – she spent most of her time lying in any sheltered area she could find.

During those long, idle hours, she would often think about her life in the hut. The Man's words remained inside her, like dormant seeds under the winter snow. She would remember the fire of the stove, the blowing wind, the long days spent talking on the rug.

There was so much the Man knew!

And how few of these things did she understand back then?

Too young were her ears, too inexperienced her heart.

The Man had often loved to challenge her with a riddle. One in particular had lingered in her mind.

'What's the difference between a pebble and a seed?'

'The pebble is heavier!' she had replied.

The Man had burst out laughing.

'The seed has a future, which the pebble does not!'

Now the Tiger knew. Seeds and thoughts were equally alive; they could wait years for life to grow inside them.

Sometimes, when the sky was obscured by autumn clouds, the Tiger would find herself overwhelmed by a slight melancholia. If only she had managed to save the Man at least! He had sacrificed his life for her, but she hadn't managed to do the same for him. She should have slaughtered his three murderers before they had even had the chance to speak. But she was too fearful, too inexperienced.

She had waited. Too long.

And he had died.

'There is no malice in you,' the Man had told her one evening. 'You're not able to see the evil around you.'

'Is that a good thing?'

'It is a gift. And, like any other gift, it is also a burden.'

Her burden was not having been able to save his life. Not being able to see or imagine evil compromised any battle. It meant always being defeated by the powers that rule the world.

Sometimes the Tiger regretted not dying as well on that fateful day. If only the bullet had been a real bullet that had pierced her heart just like the Man's! Instead, she had been forced to live.

'This bloody beast is worth more alive than dead!' the murderers had said.

Is that a curse? she wondered. *Or did that too have some sort of hidden meaning?*

'No berry falls from a bush without a reason, nor a leaf, and neither does a single hair of your fur.'

How many times had she heard him repeat this phrase during their walks?

'Who decides that?' she asked him one day, with all the boldness of her youth.

'The invisible.'

'What I cannot see?'

'What nobody can see.'

'Nobody sees it but it's there? Is this a riddle?'

'Think of the wind: who can see the wind? And your breath? Does that mean that storms don't exist then? Or that you don't exist?'

That night, after they had dined in the warmth of the hut, the Man had taken a walnut and she had watched as he cracked it open.

'This is Time,' he had said, showing her the kernel. Then he had pointed at the shell: 'And this is Eternity!'

'Is one inside the other?'

'We are inside Time, but Time is encased by Eternity. It's Eternity that creates us; it's Eternity that welcomes us at the end of our days.'

'How do you know if you can't see it?'

'Because the place you left is the place you long to go back to. Nostalgia is the imprint that Eternity leaves inside our hearts.'

Lying on the rug, as the last embers quietly died in the stove, the Tiger had stared at him.

'Was it our destiny to meet?'

'Yes,' the Man had replied, wrapping himself in his blanket.

The Tiger had one more question she wanted to ask him.

'Do those who find each other inside the kernel also find each other in the shell?'

But the Man had turned over, sinking into a deep sleep.

CHAPTER TWENTY-ONE

The Young Ibex

After a while, the snow descended on the scree too. The sun now appeared for shorter and shorter amounts of time and the moon dominated the sky, illuminating the surrounding landscape with its cold rays. Herds of large, horned prey climbed down the rocks towards the valley.

The blanket of snow had restored dignity to the Tiger's gait; the soft, powdery frost beneath her paws gave her a feeling of new-found youth.

She was growing tired of eating only marmots.

So, one morning, shortly before dawn, the Tiger crouched down behind some low fir trees. She didn't have to wait long before a herd appeared. In just three jumps she caught up with the creature lagging behind the others. She was already upon it and was about to tear it into pieces when she heard a feeble voice.

'Spare me!'

Was it possible that the prey had spoken?

At that moment, the Young Ibex turned his head, and their eyes met. His eyes were dark, velvety, staring at her with long lashes covered with tiny icicles.

'Was it you who spoke?' the Tiger asked.

The Young Ibex lowered his eyes. 'Yes.'

'I've never heard my food talking before!'

'Maybe you never wanted to listen,' a voice behind him said.

The Tiger looked around and saw a large female ibex standing nearby, watching the whole scene with fear. All the other members of the herd had run away but she stood there, legs slightly bent and horns pointed at the Tiger, as if ready to charge.

The Tiger suddenly felt a strange uneasiness. 'Do you want to challenge me?' she dared her.

The Ibex Mother shook her head. 'It's not a battle I could win.'

'What do you want then?'

'Let him live! His mouth is still wet with my milk.'

'He was too slow. The slowest creature ends up in my jaws.'

'Maybe you are the one who's too fast.'

The Tiger felt the Young Ibex trembling wildly under her front paws.

'Only the eagles have the right to prey on our young. You do not belong to our world,' the Ibex Mother insisted.

There was a long silence.

Up above them, some crows that were circling started cawing.

The Tiger had never had to make such a decision before. When she was hungry, she had to kill. Such was the law of nature.

The Ibex Mother seemed to read her thoughts.

'Eat me if you're hungry,' she said, offering her neck.

At that, the Tiger felt a huge warmth flooding her heart. The laws of her stomach dictated one thing; the law of her heart was suggesting something else entirely.

A tiger had to be a true tiger.

But what if being a true tiger meant having to transcend her own nature? What if all the roads she had travelled were meant to lead her there, to this very moment?

The Ibex Mother was offering herself just as the Man had done.

She wanted to give her life so that her child could live.

One day, long ago in the past, had the Man not told her about the Taiga beyond the Sky, where no more blood was shed?

'Going there or not,' he had said, 'depends on the fire you kindle.'

'How do you kindle fire?' she had wondered.

'There's an icy cold fire that destroys, and a warm one that builds. Both live in our heart. It's up to us to decide which one to ignite.'

'So only one of those fires burns in the taiga where no blood is shed?' the Tiger had asked timidly.

'Exactly.' The Man had nodded. 'If it weren't so, then it would be merely a mirror of our world down here.'

How long did the Tiger and the two ibexes remain still?

The sun had already ascended beyond the Easternmost spire.

The flying crows had landed on a rock nearby, waiting patiently for something to happen.

The Tiger felt the Young Ibex's jugular pulsing rapidly beneath her paws. What a familiar sensation that was! Since the first hare she had ever hunted, endless blood had flown under her claws.

Yet, at that moment, the call of that pulse was louder than that of the blood.

To her, the beating of that little heart was the only sound in the world.

When the largest of the crows came by to claim their share, the Tiger lifted her gaze up towards the mother, then back to the child, then to the mother once more. There was courage in those eyes, and trepidation too. The same courage and the same trepidation she had seen in her own mother's eyes as she watched her daughter take her first steps outside the den.

The Tiger retracted her claws and gently lifted her paws up from the fragile body.

The Young Ibex sprang up and reached his mother at lightning speed. Their muzzles touched briefly and then they both galloped down the scree without ever looking back.

The Tiger watched them cross the snowy slopes of the pasture and finally disappear towards the woods. There, they would find the rest of their herd. There, they would find moss and lichens waiting for them, which would allow them to survive through the winter.

All of a sudden, she felt herself enveloped by a deep fatigue.

With a couple of roars, she chased off the crows that were still waiting to claim the spoils of her hunt, then slowly, and with her tail lowered, she retired into her den.

And there she remained, curled up, for a very long time.

CHAPTER TWENTY-TWO

Towards the Sky

Was it a dream or was it reality?

And would she be able to tell them apart, when it came to it? All of a sudden, she thought she heard the Little Acrobat's voice. She heard it not as a distant memory, but as if he were there, alive and present beside her in the den.

'If you want to fly, you have to climb up high!' he said.

The Tiger opened her eyes wide, shaking her head.

Nobody was there.

And even if my young friend had been there, she thought, suddenly awake, *he wouldn't be anything but disappointed.*

She had lied to him, after all. She had said to him: 'I want to fly.' But it would have been more honest just to tell him the truth: 'I want to be free.'

The Little Acrobat had opened the door of her

cage for her and yet she still had not tried to lift herself even a few inches off the ground. Being able to fly was out of the question, but she could have attempted at least a little somersault.

The Tiger felt strangely light that morning. It was as if her body had begun to transform during her long sleep.

Didn't the same thing happen with butterflies? How many times had she seen them in the forest, when she was young? The creature emerging from the tiny cocoon was completely different from the one that had entered it.

What if the law of life was precisely that, she wondered: a transformation?

What if the moment to try to fly had really come?

Her paws would never allow her to climb on bare rocks, but when crossing a snowy blanket, her steps were still those of a Queen.

The Tiger emerged from her den beneath the Big Tree, shaking herself vigorously. Yes, the time had finally arrived to resume her journey.

With her head held high and her tail straight, she started climbing up the ravine which the ibexes had descended. She should have felt weakened by the lack of food, but instead she suddenly felt strong and full of energy, just as she had as a little cub running around the taiga.

She reached the first cleft in just a few bounds.

Looking out, she realized that a new scree had opened up far below, while ahead of her was an ever-higher cleft. She leaped into the deep snow, tumbling around with the same joy she and her brother had felt when they were little.

On the third day of her climb she met an eagle. She was suspended above the Tiger, seemingly motionless, soaring on an updraught.

'Are you a tiger?' she asked from up above.

'Can't you tell?' the Tiger answered, her breath short from the exertion.

'I can, yes, but I don't understand.'

'What don't you understand?'

'What are you doing up here? This isn't your Kingdom, and there are no humans to eat here. Are you lost?'

'My whole life I've been lost, looking for my own path,' answered the Tiger as she reached a ledge and dropped to the ground, exhausted.

'Why? Your parents' path wasn't enough?'

'Not for me.'

'Impossible. The path of our parents is our own path. Following it will give us everything we need.'

As she spoke, the eagle pulled up towards the East.

'Eagle!' cried the Tiger. 'You can see everything from up above; would you tell me what lies beyond the mountains?'

The eagle turned in the direction of the Tiger.

'Beyond the mountains?' the eagle repeated. 'What do you think lies there? Beyond the mountains, there are just more mountains...*ountains*...*ountains*...'

The eagle had disappeared from view, but her words still echoed down in the valley.

'...*ountains*...*ountains*...*ountains*...'

CHAPTER TWENTY-THREE

The Dance of the Crows

After her encounter with the eagle, the Tiger began to feel weaker and weaker. Her body had become lighter as she had lost weight, but the little strength she had left was barely enough to allow her to move.

There were no more gullies ahead of her, only ledges and the occasional small shrub and spur: tiny rocky steps in the steepness of the wall. It was becoming increasingly difficult to know where her next step should be – and to muster up the energy to take it.

She often imagined herself falling down, leaving patches of fur hanging like rags on the rocky spurs.

Her struggle to focus her attention on things both close and far away lent her gaze an unexpected calm, while the hardness of the climb had rid her body of anything that wasn't necessary.

This was her path now. There was no turning back.

Nor could she stop.

More than once she lost her grip and slipped down in reality. On one occasion, she was saved by a tree that sat perched on a rock; on another, a heap of fresh snow softened the impact.

Every once in a while, the Tiger raised her head to look at the peaks that towered over her climb. On some mornings they looked as if they were within grasp of her paws; at other times they seemed impossible to reach.

The passing of time had enhanced her perception of the rising sun. Although the sunrises came day after day in regular succession, she saw each one as a wonder all its own. It seemed to her as if the light were somehow turning into matter, and that matter was fire. Perhaps the world was full of flames and fires that kept spreading in an attempt to light it up.

'Not everyone can see these fires – much less catch them,' the Man had told her one day.

Now she knew that was true. It wasn't an illusion.

Behind every life there was fire, and only that fire generated light.

One morning, as the sun shone high above the peaks, the Tiger stirred from her sleep to the sound of talons scratching on the frozen ground.

Opening her eyes, she saw a large crow by her side.

He was walking around her, slowly and composed, as if entertaining a solemn thought. In fact, he was merely trying to gauge how much time she had left.

The Tiger knew that well.

In the taiga, the crows had been her faithful companions. They had followed her everywhere, like a dark, cawing cloud, waiting impatiently to strip the flesh from her prey once she herself was satisfied. They would dive at the ground and fight fiercely among themselves for the best morsels with beaks as strong as steel. From her position of power, she had always regarded them with benevolence. Ultimately, they owed their survival to her.

The Tiger stared at the crow for a long time.

'I've been a benefactress of your kind,' she told him in a barely audible whisper.

'And for that we will be eternally grateful,' replied the crow, leaning over slightly. 'But everyone must be true to their task.'

'That's right,' the Tiger answered, feeling her eyelids growing heavy.

All of a sudden, everything seemed to blur inside her head, and she couldn't tell whether she was dreaming or if it was real. Distant images overlapped, merging with one another. The days of romping around playfully with Tiger Cub, capturing her first prey, her father's eyes, the smell of the thaw and the sharp scent of ice, the rustle of the Man's step on the snow, the emptiness of the den after her mother had left.

She felt her body quiver and then fall still.

Occasionally she shuddered, startled by a noise that was just her own voice – her voice, but also those of the Tamer and the Little Acrobat, coming in waves and mingling with the voices of those who had murdered the Man.

When she opened her eyes, the Tiger noticed that the crows were now four.

They still kept a safe distance, scampering around her. They stared at her carefully, raising and lowering their heads, like tailors intent on taking measurements for a new dress.

Have I been true to my task? she was wondering, when she felt something unsteady slip beneath her paws.

She thought she had miscalculated a jump while crossing a river that was overflowing after the thaw. Instead of leaping over to the other side she must have landed on a floating tree trunk, and now the strength of the current was dragging her downstream. The water kept creeping between her paws, making her falter. She had to use every fibre of her being to avoid being swallowed by the waves, clinging on fiercely with her powerful claws.

There must be a waterfall somewhere nearby, the Tiger thought, as she heard a roaring noise growing louder and louder.

And she was right: shortly afterwards she saw a giant wall of watery mist towering ahead of her. She had no more strength left to resist the rush towards the precipice.

'So be it!' she muttered, crouching down on the trunk.

And ahead she went, to meet her fate.

But before she could be plunged into the abyss, something unexpected happened. Instead of being sucked away by a rushing vortex, she felt herself engulfed by a soft, warm breeze that licked her muzzle and ears, slipping down her back to touch her tail, just as her mother's tongue had caressed and welcomed her into the world.

CHAPTER TWENTY-FOUR

Beyond the Breach

The first thing the Tiger noticed was the smell.
It wasn't the smell of sawdust, wet with the urine of the circus elephants, or the butyric acid molecules that revealed the presence of prey even from miles away.

Inhaling more deeply, the Tiger realized that this was not even a smell, but rather a perfume. Various essences appeared to be mingled within it. Essences that evoked a particular mood.

But what mood is it? the Tiger wondered, slowly opening her eyes.

She was still there, on the same snow-covered ridge where she had fallen asleep, sinking into those confusing dreams.

The crows had vanished, along with their footprints.

Even the snow had disappeared.

The season must have turned while I was sleeping, the Tiger thought.

Looking up, she saw the rosy light of dawn graze the highest peaks.

Everything looked crisp and perfect. Dewdrops glistened on the vegetation around her, reflecting fragments of the sky.

The Tiger lifted her head, still sniffing. She realized that the perfume carried within it the memory of the season when everything is reborn.

She herself was born in that very season, in the fleeting spring of the taiga. It was in spring that she had poked her head out of the den for the first time. It was the loudness of its colours and shapes that had welcomed her after the long twilight of her weaning.

After that, everything had been a source of amazement to her. There were so many types of herbs and berries in the world! And the birds brooded their eggs in their nests under the bushes with such keen dedication!

At that time, there was a lightness in her heart. She playfully chased her own tail or Tiger Cub, or the butterflies and the large bugs that populated the taiga.

That's it, thought the Tiger. *Although I didn't know it at the time, the grace of the acrobat was already inside me.*

Forgetting your own innocence.
Could there ever be a bigger mistake?

The Tiger noticed that there was a gap in the wall of rock ahead. The gap was neither too wide nor too narrow. It seemed to have been made just for her.

How was it possible that she hadn't seen it before?

It had probably been covered by snow, or perhaps her eyesight wasn't as good as it used to be.

What lay beyond that gap in the wall?

It could be simply one of those niches carved into the rock, beyond which she would find yet another wall to come up against. Or it could be a hidden passage, like the tunnel that connected her trailer to the circus ring.

Although she felt very tired, the Tiger decided to get up.

She wanted to find out what lay beyond that wall.

Strangely, her body and legs obeyed without complaining. She knew she had lost a lot of weight, but she hadn't thought she had lost that much.

She could feel the fresh earth beneath her paws, so this could not be a dream.

She really was walking.

What if this is how the acrobats feel? she found herself thinking.

But before she could give herself an answer, she had passed through the wall.

What appeared before her eyes was neither a glacier nor a ridge, but another valley similar to that which she had left behind – only here there were no mountain ranges on the horizon to mark its borders.

It was more than a valley; this was a huge pasture with rolling hills and hollows. The grass seemed to contain all the shades of green on Earth; brushed by a light breeze, it swayed softly, like waves on the sea.

The Tiger stopped, hesitating.

Will I be allowed in? she wondered.

She saw a herd of deer pass by, not far from her. They walked proudly with their majestic jagged horns, with no sign of fear in their velvety eyes. Even a cub could attack them at this range, the Tiger thought, realizing as she did so that she was no longer hungry.

She was captivated by their beauty.

Throughout her life, she had only ever chased their backs or lunged at their throats. She had never realized how proud and noble they were.

The deer stared at her for a moment, then continued on their way.

I wonder if they see in me what I see in them, she thought, letting them pass by unharmed.

And yet she still couldn't bring herself to go in.

It was only when she saw the sun that she found the courage.

Held within that sun were all the sunrises and the sunsets she had admired in her life, and yet it looked so different from the sun she had always known. Instead of rising on one side and setting on the other, it sat unmoving in the sky.

A huge sphere, the colour of fire.

Its rays seemed to penetrate every piece of matter; they did not scorch or burn, but instead painted all things with the mild sweetness of the dawn.

The sun was calling to her, like it had called to her in the taiga.

It was that sun that encouraged her to take her first steps into the unknown pasture, discovering a vast array of flowers hidden among the tall grass. None of them had wilted or been bent; it was as if no herd had ever passed through there, as if no one had ever grazed upon them.

She looked at the flowers, then, lifting her muzzle, stared at the sky.

And in the sky, beyond the sun, she saw the stars.

She could see both the daylight and the darkness of the night. They merged into one another, as the rhythm of breathing merges with every creature called to life.

The flowers were stars, and the stars were flowers. They were reflected in one another, shining with the same splendour.

As she moved slowly forward, the Tiger realized there were several animals in the pasture, but, strangely, none of them ran away.

There no longer appeared to be predators or prey.

Every creature walked with the calm confidence of a tiger who feels like a true tiger. The same calm, the same majesty. Even the squirrels and hares. Even the clumsy marmots carried themselves with the dignity of a King or Queen.

While she was observing this strange phenomenon, the Tiger was joined by a doe. Their eyes met, and once again, the Tiger realized she was no longer hungry – only very thirsty.

Too much time had passed since she had had anything to drink. She remembered her mother's words: 'The larger prey always go to the river.'

She decided to trustingly follow the doe.

They proceeded quietly through the tall grass, strolling side by side towards the hills. When they passed the second hill, the Tiger heard the murmur of a brook in the distance. They leaned over and saw the water in a small ravine not far away.

Aside from a lamb that seemed to be resting, its legs folded underneath its body, there was no one else around.

So they descended down the slope. The grass beside the water was soft.

Once they reached the brook, the doe lowered her neck, bent her legs slightly and started drinking in small sips.

The Tiger crouched down too, like she had done as a cub, taking her time. She let her paws dangle down the bank and leaned over, dipping her tongue into the water.

What a wonderful feeling!

She had finally found some water that could quench her burning thirst!

As she drank, however, the Tiger became aware of something odd. The brook seemed to have no bottom. There were no rocks or sand, no fish or weeds in sight. Beyond the water there was only more water, just as beyond the sky there is simply more sky.

The brook seemed to slice the world in two, like a knife.

In two halves; in two lives.

For a moment, the Tiger thought she had seen her mother's face reflected next to her own. She had the same proud and joyful look that she had had when she gave birth to her.

That joy suddenly became her own.

She leaned a little further forward, stretching out a paw to try to grab the reflection. To touch her mother's fur once more – to hear her voice. To see the Man's hands again – to catch his eye.

What sort of water could it be that it seemed to contain everything she had loved?

The more the Tiger looked into the water, the more she realized how much it resembled a gemstone.

One evening, a long time before, the Man had told her about those precious stones.

'They're such wonderful gems that they radiate splendour. Everything is reflected and renewed on their surface. There are some that are coloured and others that are transparent, like diamonds. Men are willing to condemn themselves to hell just to possess them. Imagine the peace that would reign in the world if they knew that the only gems to treasure are the ones that shine from the beginning and for all eternity within their hearts.'

At that moment, the Tiger felt a voice vibrate inside her like a roar of thunder.

'Tiger!'

She jumped in surprise. Whoever could call her name with such power?

The lamb was the only creature in sight.

Then she turned around.

And saw.

The Siberian tiger, otherwise known as the Amur tiger, is one of the largest members of the cat family. These tigers were once found throughout Russia, eastern Mongolia, China and North Korea. By the 1940s, however, they were faced with extinction; in little over a century, the world had lost 97% of its tiger population, and the total number of Siberian tigers living in the wild reached as low as forty.

Although they are still seriously endangered, with the help of worldwide conservation and anti-poaching efforts, global numbers of tigers have now risen to just under four thousand, over five hundred of which are Siberian tigers. In June 2017, the World Wide Fund for Nature (WWF) launched an appeal to highlight the disastrous effects of habitat destruction and climate change, in the hope that by the next Chinese Year of the Tiger, 2022, numbers of tigers in the wild will surpass six thousand.

Find out about the many ways you can support efforts to protect the Siberian tiger here:

www.worldwildlife.org/species/amur-tiger

Oneworld, Many Voices

Bringing you exceptional writing from around the world

The Unit by Ninni Holmqvist (Swedish)
Translated by Marlaine Delargy

Twice Born by Margaret Mazzantini (Italian)
Translated by Ann Gagliardi

Things We Left Unsaid by Zoya Pirzad (Persian)
Translated by Franklin Lewis

Revolution Street by Amir Cheheltan (Persian)
Translated by Paul Sprachman

The Space Between Us by Zoya Pirzad (Persian)
Translated by Amy Motlagh

The Hen Who Dreamed She Could Fly by Sun-mi Hwang (Korean) Translated by Chi-Young Kim

The Hilltop by Assaf Gavron (Hebrew)
Translated by Steven Cohen

Morning Sea by Margaret Mazzantini (Italian)
Translated by Ann Gagliardi

A Perfect Crime by A Yi (Chinese)
Translated by Anna Holmwood

The Meursault Investigation by Kamel Daoud (French)
Translated by John Cullen

Minus Me by Ingelin Røssland (YA) (Norwegian)
Translated by Deborah Dawkin

Laurus by Eugene Vodolazkin (Russian)
Translated by Lisa C. Hayden

Masha Regina by Vadim Levental (Russian)
Translated by Lisa C. Hayden

French Concession by Xiao Bai (Chinese)
Translated by Chenxin Jiang

The Sky Over Lima by Juan Gómez Bárcena (Spanish)
Translated by Andrea Rosenberg

A Very Special Year by Thomas Montasser (German)
Translated by Jamie Bulloch

Umami by Laia Jufresa (Spanish)
Translated by Sophie Hughes

The Hermit by Thomas Rydahl (Danish)
Translated by K.E. Semmel

The Peculiar Life of a Lonely Postman by Denis Thériault
(French) Translated by Liedewy Hawke

Three Envelopes by Nir Hezroni (Hebrew)
Translated by Steven Cohen

Fever Dream by Samanta Schweblin (Spanish)
Translated by Megan McDowell

The Postman's Fiancée by Denis Thériault (French)
Translated by John Cullen

Frankenstein in Baghdad by Ahmed Saadawi (Arabic)
Translated by Jonathan Wright

The Invisible Life of Euridice Gusmao by Martha Batalha
(Brazilian Portuguese) Translated by Eric M. B. Becker

The Temptation to Be Happy by Lorenzo Marone
(Italian) Translated by Shaun Whiteside

Sweet Bean Paste by Durian Sukegawa (Japanese)
Translated by Alison Watts

They Know Not What They Do by Jussi Valtonen (Finnish)
Translated by Kristian London